Richard Doddridge Blackmore

Christowell, a Dartmoor Tale

Vol.1

Richard Doddridge Blackmore

Christowell, a Dartmoor Tale
Vol.1

ISBN/EAN: 9783337024291

Printed in Europe, USA, Canada, Australia, Japan

Cover: Foto ©Andreas Hilbeck / pixelio.de

More available books at **www.hansebooks.com**

A Dartmoor Tale.

BY

R.ᵈ D.ᵒ BLACKMORE,

AUTHOR OF "MARY ANERLEY," ETC.

"Splendidè mendax."

IN THREE VOLUMES.
VOL. I.

LONDON:

SAMPSON LOW, MARSTON, SEARLE & RIVINGTON,

CROWN BUILDINGS, 188, FLEET STREET.

1882.

CONTENTS OF VOL. I.

CHRISTOWELL.

CHAPTER I.

FAIR FLOWERS.

In the fresh young vigour of an April sun, the world has a cheerful aspect, and is doubly bright, and vastly warmer, when beheld through good flint-glass. Especially while the east winds hold, which never now forget to hold the spring of England, heart and throat. But forty years ago, there were some springs of gentle quality.

Upon a pleasant April morning, of the sweet inconstant kind, such as we vainly sigh for now, a gardening man, with a quick step, came into his happy greenhouse. A door from his favourite sitting-room led into this still more favoured place; and the smile with which he entered showed that he expected to find pleasure here.   It was a long, low, span-roof house, with no side-lights, and very simple, not even framed with rafters.   Yet snug from violence of wind, and bright with every sunbeam; this humble house was rich with joy, for all who love good health, and peace.

Here, were the sweet obedience, and the gay luxuriance of the vine; than which no lovelier creature grows.   Broad leaves, spreading into pointrels, waved and cut with crisp indenture, coving into, or overlapping, the ripple of each other; clear round shoots, cresting up like swans, and sparkling with beads of their own breath; infant bunches, on the bend as yet, but promising to straighten, as the berries got their weight; some bravely announcing grapes already, some hoping to do so before nightfall, through the misty web of bloom; others only just awaking into eyes of golden dust; yet all alike rejoicing, shining, meeting the beauty of the early sun, and arousing their own to answer it.

And here was a multitude of pretty things as well, that will not be chambered with the vine too long, yet gladly accept a kind lift upon the road from winter to summer, which her auspice yields. Boxes, and little tubs, and pots, and pans, and frames of willow, and biscuit-cases, were cropped with growth in different stages, and of divers orders, through all the innumerable tones of green, and all the infinite variety of form. But all, to the keenest human eye, brisk, and clean, and in their duty.

The man, who had shaped these things, and led them (under the Maker's loftier will) was coming to them now, with a cheerful heart, and faith in his own handiwork. The finest gardener, that ever grew, knows well that he cannot command success, and has long survived young arrogance. Still he continues to hope for the best; for the essence of the gentle craft is hope, rooted in labour, and trained by love. So this man took a short taste of the air, glanced at the glass, and the glitter of the vines, and felt the climate of the house, as keenly as if he were a plant therein. For the moment, there was no fault to find. Genial warmth was in the air, and gentle dew on every leaf; in the slope of early sun through glass, no harsh heat quivered, and no fierce light glared; but morning-tide spread all soft herbage with a silvery tissue.

"Now I like to see things look like this,"

said the man, as he very well might say; "but here are at least a score of bunches crying aloud for the thinning scissors. And where is Rose, who ought to be at them, before the sun gets up too high? Rose of roses, where are you?"

To his cheerful shout no answer came; and being of a well-contented mind, he went on to his own business. His happy nature found its province in promoting happiness, whether of beast, or bird, or life whose growth is its only movement. To all of these he felt that loving-kindness, which is nature's gift; not the brightest of her graces, but the largest, and the best. Without that one redeeming gift. of which grand intellects often fail, this man being sorely tried in life. would have passed into the bitter vein, so miserable to itself, and all. His face had the lines of resolute will, and of strenuous energy; and his bodily force was but little abated by three score years of exercise. For his back was as straight as a soldier's on drill; his legs were stout and steadfast; and although he fed well, and without anxiety, none but envious whipper-snappers would have dared to call him fat.

For the other part, his mind was not disagreeably large or noble; but just in front. by the proper peg, of the general mind it met with. The general mind, that is to say, of educated people, at any rate in that part of the world, which is as wise as any other. "Captain Larks" (as this good stranger had been called by the native voice, when first he came to Christowell) was a simple, unpretentious man, who gave himself no title. His only desire seemed to be for plain life, and retirement.

These he surely might here obtain, to the utmost of all heart's desire; so far away was Christowell from busy mart, or town, or street, or even road of carriage power. No better place could have been discovered by a man sincerely desirous of dealing as little as possible with mankind. For here were people enough to make a single head no rarity; yet not enough to force any sort of head into grievous eminence. All the inhabitants, without exertion, were important enough to feel satisfied; or at any rate to feel the duty of it; while universal opinion stopped any man from indulging in his own. It may be denied by young spread-eagles, of competitive and unruly mind, that this is the highest form of human life. But such an one should soar aloft, and perch upon some higher one.

To Christowell, ambition was no more than a longer name for itch. Every village-man grew wiser by due seniority; and no mind, while its father lived, succeeded to authority. Youth was kept in its place, and taught that the ear must take the seed of thought, until the white hair shows it ripe; and women were allowed their proper weight.

"Christowell is all very well," the gardener went on thinking; "but if ever there was a slow place under the sun, it is one of the slowest. Pugsley will never bring my pots."

Making up his mind to the manner of mankind, with a cultivator's patience, he passed beneath clusters encroaching on the headway, and went into a tiny transept, parted from the rest of the house, by a narrow door of glass. Here was a separate shrine for flowers, intolerant of heat, and demanding air, beyond the young vine's capacity. Choice geraniums lived here, and roses, heaths, and epacrids, and double violets, lilies of the valley (sweetest of all bloom), Daphne, and the graceful deutzia, pansies also, freaked with velvet braid, the double black polyanthus, and the white chalice of azalea. But best, and dearest of all to him, and set in a separate nook—as in a glazed bureau with lifting glass—that exquisite flower of exclusive worship, that gorgeous instance of nature and art combined to do their utmost, the magically beautiful auricula.

No gardener is worth his manure, who has not a fine conceit of his own skill. " I should like to have some of those Lancashire fellows, or a few of those Kentish braggarts here," this man said aloud, being apt to encourage his thoughts, when alone, with the company of words; " if I know anything of the matter, this green-edged seedling, beautifully named ' Dartmoor Oasis,' by my Rose; and this grand self, one could gaze at all the day; and above all this white-edge, this glorious white-edge, worthily entitled ' Cream of Devon,'—have they anything fit to hold a candle to them? Consider the paste, take the measure of the thrum, dwell upon the band; can you spy a single slur? Above all, if you have a particle of judgment, observe the equality of the pips, the perfection of fulness, and true circle of the truss, and the grand, columnar, mealy, magnificent, staunchly upright, and splendidly proportioned—really you might say, pillar of the stalk!"

Overpowered, alike by his eloquence, and the beauty that produced it, he stopped for a moment, with some gravel in his hand (with which he was going to top-dress his pots), when the little door was opened, and his Rose came in; whose presence, might compel the wildest gardener to despise his own auriculas.

CHAPTER II.

To a mind with limited powers of inquiry, such as most of us are blest with, a great truth stands forth in robust relief, without being bound to show what it stands on, or where it came from, or anything else. In this frank spirit must be accepted the incontestable fact that "Latham" (an ancient and very good surname) takes, upon the ordinary tongue of Devon, the brief, but still excellent form of "Larks." It made no difference, from their lofty point of view, that the Captain's name was not "Latham" at all, any more than he called himself a captain ; but when he first appeared among the natives of this part—some fifteen years ago perhaps—his rather scanty luggage was ticketed "L. Arthur," in flowing and free manuscript. The leading genius of Christowell—a premature intellect now removed

from the stabs of contumely, to higher claims—
pronounced at a glance that the word spelled
" Latham ; " whilst some, almost equally capable
of reading, confessed, and some denied it.

The landlord of the *Three Horse-shoes*, who
could not sign his name (though he drew
three horse-shoes, at the bottom of a bill, more
correctly than many an artist could), at once
backed up the decision of the wit, and settled
the question, by declaring that his guest had
the very same walk, all over the world, as
Corporal Larks to Teigncombe had. So before
Mr. Arthur was one dinner-time older, he came
forth upon the public as " Captain Larks ; " and
finding that people only shook their heads, and
looked very knowing, if he said another word,
he let them have their way, until his ears
and mind grew used to it.

Through an agent at Exeter, whose name
was " Tucker," a neat little cottage, and some
twenty acres of land near the moor, had been
bought for him cheaply. Then the cottage
was furnished very simply ; and here he hoped
to spend in peace, and solitude, his remaining
days.

As yet, there was not a grey hair on his
head, though his face bore marks of evil climate,

and uncourteous usage, in deep-grained sun-
burn, and scar of steel, permanent in three
places. This, and a pair of shaggy eyebrows,
gave him a formidable aspect, much against
the meaning of his mind. But eyes of a soft
bright blue, as clear as a child's, and a nose
of genial turn, and a really pleasant and hearty
smile, showed plenty of good-will towards mankind, whatever man might have done to him.
Moreover, his large and well-knit frame, active
step, and resolute bearing, commanded the good
word of womankind, the better half of the
entirety.

Then Parson Short, becoming now prime
minister of Christowell, said his say about
Captain Larks, which was to the purpose, as
usual. "Under a cloud—fine fellow by his
face—gentleman, according to his speech and
manner. He wants to be quiet; it is none of
our business. Let him alone, till he comes
to us."

The settler asked for nothing better than
this course of treatment. The stir of his arrival
soon settled, like himself, into gentle quietude;
the men of the village were kind and respectful
—as men still are in Devonshire—and the
women, though longing to know more about

him, felt for him deeply as "the lonely gentle-man," and hoped he would get over it, and have another wife.

Whatever his trouble, he sought no pity, nor even appeared despondent; but lived upon his bit of land, and worked, and whistled among his trees, as sweetly as the blackbirds that came to answer. In spite of his maturity, or perhaps by reason of it, many a village girl, too young to dream of any courting—except in dim wonder at the number of the babies—resolved to be his wife, as soon as time should qualify her, and came up the steep hill, every fine evening, to peep through the hedge at him, and perhaps to get an apple. He, having love of children, as of all things that are natural, would rest from his work, and come out at the stile, and pat their curly heads, and ask the history of the babies, and cut for them chips, with his pruning-knife, from a big stick of liquorice in his waistcoat pocket.

Whether he had kith or kin, or any soft belongings, was a moot point at the Church-yard gate, and by many smouldering peat-fires; until, about four years after his coming, a lively, and lovely, little girl was delivered at his gate, by Tim Pugsley, the carrier. Tim went round about it, as a fox goes to his hole, and avoided the village on his way from Moreton; but in spite of all that, they were spied by a woman with a bundle of furze at the top of the cleve; and when human nature, with five shillings in its pocket, compelled Master Pugsley to pull up and bait, at the *Three Horse-shoes*, upon his homeward course, he had no call so much as to change his crown; so liberal was the desire to treat him, for the sake of the light that he could shed. The grateful carrier first drank his beer, then shook his head, as vehemently as if it had been labelled " glass with care; " and then enlightened the company with a piece of news beyond all price—" Every man should first tend his own business."

For nine or ten years, every summer, and weighing more upon each delivery, this consignment came to pass; and Pugsley (like his cart-tilt, which was of some high new patent stuff) grew dryer and dryer, every time he was wetted; till Christowell understood at last, that if anybody was to blame, for keeping the parish so unsettled, it was no less a person than the famous Bishop of Exeter. For Pugsley told them to go to the bishop, if they wanted to know all the rights; and the next confirmation in that neighbourhood was largely attended by fathers and mothers. It did them good to be confirmed again, because of their principles wearing out; and the landlord of the inn was pleased with the evening they spent after it.

Thus when Rose came down at last, "to have holiday for ever" (as she told Mr. Pugsley, every time he stopped to put a stone behind the wheel), there was scarcely any one in Christowell old enough to rejoice, who failed of that most Christian duty. The captain for once came out of his garden, and made a great bonfire of his weeds upon the beacon, and with his own hands rolled up a great barrel of cider unknown to the natives, whose ignorance culminated towards their heads. For he now grew apples of a lordly kind, which they (having faith in their grandsires only) disdained, till it turned the tables on them.

Almost everybody said, that night, or else on the following morning, that for certain sure, such a lively maid could never abide in a place like that. Or if she did, she must soon go doiled—so tarble weist, and crule unkid as it was. For according to the way Captain Larks held his head up, in spite of demeaning himself now lately, his daughter must count upon having to behave like a lady, and not going to and fro, and in and out with the other young folk, as the butcher's, and grocer's girls might do.

And who was there likely to ask her in marriage, or to take her to dance, or a fairing, or a club, comely as she was, and so nice-spoken? Why, Parson Tom Short was the only gentry-man, unless you went so far as Touchwood Park; and if ever there was a set bachelor in the world, Parson Short was one of them; let alone that his hair was all going from his poll, and his cook, Mrs. Aggett, would have no young doings.

Up to the present time, however, though nearly two years were gone by, Rose Arthur had complained to no one, of discontent, or loneliness. Her father, and her work, and books, sufficed to her for company; and her lively nature filled itself with interest in all things. She knew everybody in the village now, and every flower in the garden; and her father's lonely life was blessed by her young enjoyment of the world.

Pugsley (who lived at Moreton, and traded twice a week from Exeter, when the weather and the roads encouraged him) now began to find his horse wink one eye, at the turn towards Christowell. So many trifles went to and fro, and some boxes that made the axle creak, and some quite large enough to sit upon. Even before this, he had taken mauns of plants, and baskets of choice pears, and grapes, to Exeter; when the captain began to " demean " himself in the village esteem by traffic. But now the commerce increased, and throve, as Rose threw her young life into it.

If Pugsley had been a small-minded man, he must have gone promptly to Tavistock fair, and bought a new horse, to attend to this traffic; for his ancient nag, whose name was " Teddy," began to find the hills grow steeper, as the weight of years increased. But the carrier was of gentle tone, and largely generous sentiments; and hours of reflection made him wipe his head with loftier feeling. Therefore he would not deny his good neighbours the pleasure of bene-volence, but allowed them to lend him a horse as often as they wished, and sometimes oftener.

Now Teddy was crawling up the hill, that beautiful April morning, with the long-desired load of pots. Three-quarters of a mile of jagged lane, or sometimes of roaring watercourse, led from the village to " Larks' Cot," as irreverent people called it. At best, and even for a fresh young horse, it was a tough piece of collar-work ; but Teddy, ancient though he was, would never have grumbled, if the lane had been wide enough for corkscrew. But in this part of Devon, the rule of the road is, to make it just wide enough for one cart, and a cow to go past it without losing milk. If two carts meet, one must back to a gateway; and whether of the twain shall back, depends upon the issue which of the drivers is " the better man."

Therefore this Teddy had a hard time of it— a long pull, a stong pull, and worst of all, a straight pull. And while he was pausing, to pant, and to think, and his master whistled softly, Jem Trickey the cobbler came merrily down a steep place, and stopped to look at them.

" Marnin' to 'e, Tim," shouted Trickey, for his breath was as " plim " as a football newly filled ; " what have 'e got then, this time, carryer ? "

" No consarn of thine, Cobbler Trickey ; " Pugsley made stout answer, being cross, and short-fetched in the wind ; " cobblers is not excisemen yet."

" Potses, and panses again, as sure as I be a zinner ! Cappen Larks ought to be shamed of hiszelf. Lor' A'mighty never made his works to grow in crockery. And you'm a gwain outside your trade. Backard and forrard is your proper coorse. Let me conzeider of they potses."

"Ye be welcome to conzeider of them, cobbler. A niver zeed sich coorous cloam. Look'e yeer, they little holes hurneth all round 'em! Cappen's own diskivry, I do hear tell."

The carrier loosened the cord of one crate, and allowed the intelligent Trickey to gaze, while he drew it towards the cart-tail. Trickey, though large enough of mind, was small of body; and he lifted himself by the lade, to see things justly.

"You be bound by my advice," he cried, retreating hastily; "you take the next turn down to brook, and heft they into the watter. They was made for the witches, and no mistakk about 'em."

"Zo I wull," Tim Pugsley answered, pretending to share his neighbour's fright, for he was a dry man, and full of book-learning. "Thank'e kindly for thy counsel, Jem. Into the watter they gooth, zure enough. Only thou must pay for the vally of 'em, and the carryage too, Cobbler Trickey."

"Go thy way with thy witchcraft," the other replied. "Do 'e know what I call thee, Carryer Pugsley? I call thee a poor time-sarver, and a carryer of no conzistency."

"I carry better stuff than thou dost," Pugsley shouted after him; as the shoe-maker, with a springy step, set off down the hill, for fear of worse. "Do I zwindle the public with brown papper? Do I putt 'ooden pegsin, and zwear they be stitched? Do I clam on the heel-ball, to hide my scamping? Do I——"

Master Pugsley cut short his list of libels, as he saw Master Trickey, at a decent distance, deliver a gesture of supreme contempt, by turning up his coat-tail, and administering a slap to the quarter of his body which was latest in retreat.

"Do 'e do the like of that to I?" the carrier inquired superfluously; "If it twadn't for business, and the blessed law—howsomever, a bain't worth thinking on; Teddy, gee wugg! It be your vault mainly."

The old horse, wont as he was to bear the blame of troubles far outside of his own shafts, rallied with a shiver and a rattle of his chains, and threw himself forward upon the strain. For a very stiff tug arose just here, for a horse

who had been to Exeter and back, with a tidy
load, only yesterday; and whose knowledge of
corn was too superficial, getting more of the
husk than the kernel for its study. And the
manner of a Devonshire lane is such, that
dogmatic humps stand up, in places, where
nothing seems to warrant them. The meadows,
to the right and left, may be as pleasant as you
please to walk upon, with a sleek benevolence,
a velvet pile, and a spring of supple freshness.
And yet, within a landyard the lane is jumping
scraggily, with ribs of solid rock, and pits and
jags of bold abruptness. The nag, being born
to such conditions, plodded on without repining;
but in spite of all spirit, and skill, and care,
he suddenly fell into sad disgrace.

For just as the near wheel was creaking, on
the verge of a steep slide of granite, where his
turn-about was due—for the lane there allowed
him chance of a little bit of slanting—Teddy
did a thing that any other horse might do, or
even a man in his position. He mistook a large
stone-fly, just arisen from the Christow, for a
genuine œstrus, a bot-fly, whame, or tabanus.
If he had thought of the present time of year,
he must have known better; but instead of
thinking, he acted on his nerves, which struck

into him like a spur. Up went his head, as if he were four years old, instead of going on for forty; and his old bones shook with indignation, at the pestilent state the world was come to. "Steady, you old fool! Who'm a-gwain for to kill'e?" the carrier exclaimed with a little friendly thump; but the mischief was done, while he was speaking. For the jump of the horse gave a jerk to the shaft, and this ran amiss into the axle-tree, gave a lollop to the near wheel, already on the wamble; and down went the felly, with a blue grind of iron, into the very hole they meant to shun. The hole was more than deep enough to hold a good nine gallons; and the wheel ground down into its deepest depth, while the other took advantage of the position for a holiday, and proved itself the off-wheel, by going off towards heaven.

"Wull now!" said the carrier, without much haste, for his mind travelled slowly up the obstacles of thought; "this be a tarble dicky-ment; and here coom'th arl the cloam! Drat that old cobbler chap, 'twor arl his doings."

An avalanche of pots, from the unroped crate, fell around him and upon him, while he reasoned thus. Like a quick shower of acorns from the shaken oak, but alas, much heavier, and more valuable, they rattled on the carrier, and thumped his poor chest, and a far more tender and impassioned part of man, till he fairly turned back, and let them roll upon his spine.

"Jem, neighbour Jem, do'e come back, that's a dear;" he shouted, as loud as his drummed condition furnished, to the cobbler in the distance at the bottom of the hill. That good neighbour not only heard him, but replied right pleasantly, with a gladsome laugh, and a smart repetition of his gay defiance; then hastened on his course, with a step more nimble than his customers generally could compass from his shoes.

"All men is clay," said the carrier, recovering his native equanimity, and wiping the red dust from his fustian suit; "all men is clay; and the Lord hath not intended us to putt His material into these here shapes, with a C. R. upon 'em, maning carrier's risk. Wull, a carn't brak' no more of 'un nor there be, now can 'e, Teddy? Smarl blame to thee, old chap. We'll both of us toorn to our brexass. This hosebird job hath coom, I rackon, 'long of doing of despite to the gifts of the Lord."

Beholding a very nice place to sit down, and content with the cart in its present firm fixture, he pulled out the nosebag, and buckled it for Teddy, so that he might cast one eye down at his lip-service. Then he drew forth his own provender, and seasoned it, by dwelling on its beauties with his broad brown thumb. " Nation good, nation good ! " he could not help exclaiming ; " a good waife is the making of a man's front-piece. A vartuous woman laveth no occasion for a man to think twice of his vitteling, or zeek to read the papper. Best use of papper is to putt up bakkon in 'un."

Sorrow, and breakage, and the other plagues of life, began to use less and less of pressure on his heart, as he sat upon a lady-fern (not yet plumed for dancing, but rich with soft beauty for a heavy man to sit upon) and biting out the cork from a flat stone bottle, moistened down the roadway for the bread and meat to follow. Then he fell to very heartily, and in less than half an hour began to feel nicely refreshed, and fit to encounter the issue before him.

CHAPTER III.

PARSON SHORT.

"I AM almost sure that he must have broken down," said the fairest of his flowers to the gardener; "he is the most punctual man in the county, and scarcely ever more than three days late. I saw him not more than three miles off, on the top of the hill above Lustleigh, before the sun was three yards high; and he must have been here, wiping his head, as a delicate hint for cider, two hours ago, if he had gone on well."

"Perhaps he has gone on too well, my dear, by taking the turn to the *Three Horse-shoes*. Not that I would cast any slur upon your pet; but still such things will happen."

"To other people perhaps they might. But never to him—I am quite sure of that. The last time I saw him, he lamented cordially 'the mischief of them publics.'"

" That was very good of him, and showed high principle, as well as a tender conscience," Mr. Arthur replied, while he took good care that his daughter should not observe his smile ; for life enough was before her yet, for correction of faith in human nature. " Pugsley has the elements of a lofty character, industry, honesty, philosophy—in the sense of that word at present."

" Father," cried Rose, having finished her bunch, and running up to him, with the long grape-scissors in her hand, and a trail of bast around her neck ; " have I got the elements of a lofty character—industry, certainly, just look at those ten bunches ; honesty, perhaps to a reasonable extent ; but scarcely a bit of philosophy, I'm afraid ? "

" Certainly not too much of that," her father answered quietly ; " but run in, and see about the breakfast, darling ; or perhaps you may discover some defects in mine."

" How I wish that I could ! But I shall never do that, if philosophy means good temper. Now come and see my work, sir, and say if it is good."

" It is good sound work ; far better than Lord Bicton's head-gardener, at any money, could produce, in vineries like a cathedral. However it is not faultless yet; though I don't mean to say, that I could do it better, even if my eyes were as young as yours. You understand thoroughly the bunch, as it is; and you shape it beautifully for the time; nothing could be neater, or more justly placed. But you have yet to learn the fine perception of the future, the bending of the footstalk, as the berries grow in weight, and the probable drop of the shoulders. And practice alone can teach you the different ins and outs of each kind of grape, in swelling."

"The subject appears to me to be endless. How shall I ever attain to such knowledge?"

"By watching the results of your own work, and by never giving over."

"Till old experience do attain to something like prophetic strain. But father, how did you thus attain it? Have you ever been apprenticed to a gardener?"

"Little pitchers may have long ears; but they must not have curious tongues!" he replied, with a kiss on her forehead, to heal the rebuke. "Now let us go to breakfast; and then seek Pugsley."

Hence it came to pass that while the good

carrier was still regarding the position of his
cart, and the attitude of his ancient horse, with
calm eyes, and well-kindled pipe, a spirited
young lady stood before him, and did not share
his patience.

" Good morning, Master Pugsley ; and you
seem to think it good. But I always have
understood, that a cart ought to stand upon both
wheels."

" So her did. You'm right there, Miss," the
carrier answered, with a quiet grin. " But there
be times when her doth'nt do her dooty, but
go'oth contrairy, like the wominvolk."

" And you mean to let her stay like that, for
ever! And my father's pots lying in a heap
upon the road ! "

" Cappen is a just man, and a' wull look auver
it. Partikler now you've zeed it, Miss, and
can sartify 'twor no hooman doin's."

" All I can certify is, that you seem content
to stay here for the rest of the day. Do please
to get out of that hole at once, and bring all the
pots you have managed not to break."

" Lor', how natteral you do spake! It doth a
man good to hear'e, Miss. Here us must baide,
nolum wolum, till sich taime as Farmer Willum
coom'th."

"Farmer William may not come at all, or at any rate not till twelve o'clock. Now do put your shoulder to the wheel yourself. I am very strong, and I will help you."

The carrier was too polite to laugh, though he cherished that disdain of female prowess, against which the chivalrous author of "Dorothy" couches his elegiac lance. But this man only puffed the pipe of silence.

"You fancy that I can do nothing, I suppose," cried Rose, who was as prickly as a moss-rose, when provoked; "but I can do a whole quantity of things, such as would quite surprise you. I can milk a cow, and pot a vine, and bed down a pony, and salt a silverside, and store apples, and fry potatoes, and fill a pipe. And if all that is nothing, as you might be apt to think, because of being a man, Mr. Pugsley, I can answer for taking a hive of bees, without hurting one of them. Can you do that?"

"The Lord forbid! He hath made 'em to be smoked, zoon as ever they a' done their work. But, Missy, it amooseth me to hear you tell up. You tell up a sight of things as a well-inventioned man can do, or if not one, mebbe then anither of 'em. But you never tak' no count on the hardest thing of arl, the like of which no man can do in this here county. You knows what I mane, Miss Rose; and winderful it is to me, for sich a babe and suckling!"

"Oh! I know what you mean quite well. You have made me do it in the cart so often. But I do assure you that it is quite easy."

"Aisy a' can never be," said the carrier decisively; "although a' zimth as some can do 'un, droo years of arly lanin'. To play the piander is winderful : but a varmer's datter may coom to that, bein' outside of her dooty; but niver can her coom to spakin' of the bad Vrench langoowich."

"I tell you, Master Pugsley, that every one can do it, in my proper rank of life. You are not stupid enough to suppose that because I pot vines——"

"Noo, noo, Miss; axing of your pardon for breaking in upon you. I knows as well as the Royal mail doth, that you be one of the karlity. None but a vule could look twice at you, and veel any doubt whatsomdever about that, my dear. And Cappen Larks, though he dooth quare things, is the very same; at any rate to my mind."

" And to everybody's mind, I should hope, Mr. Pugsley. But he must not, and he shall not be called ' Captain Larks ; ' as you know, if nobody else does. Now please to get out of your rut, and come on."

The nature truly noble, and the mind of lofty power, reluctant as they always are to make disclosure of themselves, and shunning as they always do the frippery of random praise, unwittingly are revealed sometimes by the conduct of tobacco-smoke. Shallow men, or hasty fellows, or small sons of discontent, labour hard with restless puffs, and vex the air with turbid fumes, promiscuously tossed from lip or bowl. How different is the process of the large, self-balanced, contemplative pipe! No swirling tempest battles round the brow, no waste of issue clouds the air ; but blue wreaths hover far asunder, circling placidly as they soar, like haloes round the head of peace ; the cool bowl shines without exuding, like the halcyon of the charm and calm, and sweet rest satisfies the spirit of the man, gratefully ministering the gift divine.

In a state of mind thus serene and lofty, Master Pugsley smoked his pipe. Maiden impatience stirred him not, nor the casual shords of a slight mishap, nor the general fragility of human kind. If his cart was not upon

a level axle, should that disturb his own equi-
poise? So he sat down again, in a courteous
manner, and delivered very sound advice;
while the young lady ran away, and left him
to enjoy it, for she saw that help was near at
hand.

Now a man of good sense, and strong will, led
the simple people of Christowell. In any trouble
or turning of the mind, as well as in bodily
ailments, there was not a grown-up man, or
woman, who sought to go further than Parson
Short. The Rev. Tom Short, vicar of the
parish, coming to an utterly neglected place,
had quietly made his way, by not insisting upon
it unduly. Resolute good-will, plain speech,
and fair allowance for adverse minds, together
with a comfortable income of his own, enabled
him to go on well, and to make his flock do
likewise. He addressed them "on papper"
only once a week, which was quite as much as
they required; and that they did with diffidence.
He, however, was well convinced of the mutual
duty thereby discharged. No other preacher in
the diocese could say so much in the time
allowed, which was never more than five
minutes; and no other congregation listened
with attention so close, and yawns so few.

In other matters, his style was dry, and terse, and quick to the purpose; yet seldom rough, and never arrogant or overbearing. Steadfast Tory as he was, he respected everybody's rights, and felt due sympathy for their wrongs, whenever he could see them. His education had been good at Winchester, and New College; whence he had taken high classical honours, though his college was then exempt from test. For his manner of sticking to the point at issue, and knowing nothing—unless he knew it well—was just what Oxford then encouraged. His bodily appearance was not grand, nor large, nor at all imposing; and the principal weakness of his mind was a morbid perception of that defect. Not that he could be called a dwarf, or plain, or at all unsightly; only that his spirit, being very great had a hankering for larger tenement. This feeling perhaps had saved his freedom, by making him shy of long-bodied ladies, while it kept him from admiring short ones. So now he was nearing his fortieth year, with a prospect of nothing but bachelorhood, which his cook was determined to maintain on his behalf. Yet many a young lady of exalted stature would gladly enough have become Mrs. Short.

For this was a ruddy, brisk, and very cheerful

man, bald it is true, on the top of his head, but plenteously whiskered, largely capable of beard —if clerical principles should ever close the razor, which they were beginning even now to do in London—gifted moreover with a very pleasant smile, a short waggish nose, and keen blue eyes. No better man could fill his shoes, or at any rate could get into them, so well compressed was his material, and so good the staple.

It was not only this, nor yet the graceful increment of his income, nor even the possession of a spiritual turn, that led the young ladies to be thinking of him, whenever any settlement in life was mentioned. He inspired large interest by his own merit, but a feeling yet larger and deeper, by his present sad position. To rescue him from the despotism of Mrs. Aggett, his widowed cook, was the lofty aim of almost every other female. But he bore his yoke with patience, and preferred the known to the unknown ill.

"How now, Pugsley? Stuck fast like this, and the captain's pots smashed up like that!" this bachelor shouted, as he marched up briskly, saw the position, and understood the large resignation of the native mind.

"Stuck slow, I karls it, Passon Shart. And thicky cloam be smashed, more down than oop. If her baided oop, her wud 'a been all zound."

"Come, Master Tim, get out your levers, instead of argifying."

"Passon, I wull; if so be I've got 'un. The Lord know'th, whether they be here, or to home."

"Here they are, more peart than you be;" Mr. Short replied, turning up some old rubbish from the bottom of the cart, and drawing forth two spars of ash ; "now wugg on, Teddy, when I give the word."

"No man as ever I see yet," said the carrier, through a blue ring of smoke, "hath received the power to make Teddy wugg, when a' hath his nosebag on ; avore such time, as his tongue have been into the uttermost corners of the zame."

Parson Short, without any answer, unbuckled the strap of the hairy wallet, gently withdrew it from the old fellow's nose (though he put up one foot to protect it), and marching sternly up the hill, hung this fine temptation upon a hazel bush, at the first corner. Teddy, with a whinny of soft remonstrance, pricked up his ears, and looked anxious to proceed.

"Passons has no conscience whativer," said. the carrier, pocketing his pipe; "they dis- tresses all the hanimals, like the better sort, on Zindays. Niver lets nobody baide at peace."

"Cease from weak reflections, and take to action," the inexorable Short replied. "If your time is worthless, mine is not. Stir him up, Pugsley, while I start the wheel."

"I vear your reverence be a'most too small," said Pugsley, with much good will, but touching the vicar in his most tender part. Mr. Short took off his coat, folded it carefully, and laid it on a rock-moot, because it was a very good one; then turning up shirt-sleeves of fair white linen, he showed a pair of arms as well-com- plexioned as a lady's, but thick-set, bossy, and substantial. "Lor' a' mussy," cried the carrier, "thou should'st niver have a goon on!"

Deigning no answer, the sturdy parson seized the bigger of the two ash staves, and laying the butt of the other for a fulcrum, gave the stuck wheel such a powerful heft, that the whole cart rattled, and the crates began to dance.

"Zober, passon, zober! Or ee'll heft 'un over tother zide," said Pugsley, running up

to the horse's head; "now, Teddy, taste thy
legs, and strive at 'un."

At a touch of the whip on his legs, the old
nag threw his chest out, and grappled the
ground with his hoofs.   Then he cast his
weight forward, and strained to the tug, with
his back on the stretch, and his ribs like hoops,
and even his tail stiffened up like a hawser.

"Heave-oh!" shouted Parson Short, suiting
the action to the word; "well done then, old
horse, we are out of the hole!"

CHAPTER IV.

CHRISTOWELL village (in full view of which, the horse, cart, and driver, had rested so long) affords to the places above it, or below, fair plea for contemplation. Many sweet beauties of tempered clime flower the skirts of the desolate moor, and the sweetest of these is Christowell. Even the oldest inhabitant cannot, to the best of his recollection, say, whether he ever did hear tell, that the place was accounted beautiful. He knoweth that picture-men do come, and set up three-legged things, and stand, as grave as judges, to make great maps, like them that be hanging in the schoolroom; but he never yet hath known any odds to come of it; the rocks abide the same, as if they never had been drawed, and the trees—you may look for your-self, and say whether they have fetched another apple. For when the Lord rested on Saturday night, His meaning was not, that the last of His works should fall to, and make strokes of the rest of them.

Sound sense of such lofty kind is the great gift of this village. Every man here would be contented, if he only had his due; failing of that, he keeps his merit to the mark of his wages, by doing his day's work gently. If a neighbour gets more than himself, he tries hard to believe that the man should have earned it; and even his wife is too good to declare, what she thinks of the woman next door to her. Among themselves sometimes they manage to fall out very cordially; but let anybody sleeping out of the parish, have an unbecoming word to say of his betters who are inside it, and if he walk here, without a magistrate behind him, scarcely shall he escape from the sheep-wash corner in the lower ham.

For a beautiful brook of crystal water, after tumbling by the captain's cot, makes its own manner of travelling here, rarely allowing the same things to vex it, or itself to complain of the same thing, twice. From crags, and big deserts, and gorges full of drizzle, it has scrambled some miles, without leisure for learning self-control, or patience. And then it comes suddenly, round a sharp corner, into the quiet of Christowell, whose church is the first work of man it has seen, except that audacious cottage. Then a few little moderate slips, which are nothing, compared with its higher experience, lead it with a murmur to a downright road, and a ford where men have spread it gently, and their boys catch minnows. Here it begins to be clad with rushes, and to be curbed by jutting trees, and lintelled by planks, for dear gossip and love; for cottages, on either bank, come down, and neighbours full of nature inhabit them.

Happy is the village that has no street, and seldom is worried by the sound of wheels. Christowell keeps no ceremonial line of street, or road, or even lane, but goes in and out, as the manner of the land may be, or the pleasure of the landlords. Still there is a place where deep ruts grow, because of having soft rock under them; and this makes it seem to be the centre of the village, and a spot where two carts meet sometimes; for the public-house is handy. Once upon a time, two carts met here, and here they spent a summer's day, both being driven by obstinate men, who were not at all their owners. Neither would budge from his own rut, and the horses for several hours rubbed noses, or cropped a little grass, while the men lay down. Being only first cousins, these men would not fight; as they must have done, if they had been brothers. Yet neither of them would disgrace his county—fair mother of noble stubbornness—by any mean compromise, or weak concession; so they waited until it grew dark; and then, with a whistle of good will, began to back away together, and as soon as they found room to turn, went home to supper from a well-spent day.

But such a fine treat and stir of interest was rare, and the weather was the only thing that could be trusted for supplying serious diversion. Herein nobody was wronged of subject; for the weather was so active, that the hardest-working man could spend his time in watching it. No sooner had he said that it must be fine, than ere he could catch up his spade again, it was flying in his face, and he was eating his own words. Herein alone, is variety enough to satisfy people of contented heart. For scarcely ever did the same things look the same, for two hours together.

Upon a day of well-conducted weather, beginning brightly in the morning, a stranger newly arrived from town may feed, and gaze, alternately. At sunrise, he is in bed of course; largely saving the disappointment, which the lavish promise of the east might bring. But even at eight of an average morning, when he wants his breakfast, the world is spread before him well, with soft light flowing up the plains, and tracing lines of trees, and bends of meadow. He stands, or sits down to his bacon and eggs, twelve hundred feet above sea-level, with fair land, and bright water, spreading three-fourths of the circle around him. To the east, some five leagues off, are the dark square towers of Exeter cathedral, backed by the hazy stretches of Black-down; on the right are glimpses of the estuary of Exe, from Powderham Castle towards Starcross. Outside them, and beyond, and overlapping every landmark, the broad sweep of the English Channel glistens, or darkens, with the moods above it, from the Dorset headlands to the Start itself. Before he has time to make sure of all this, the grand view wavers, and the colours blend; some parts retire, and some come nearer; and lights and shadows flow and flit, like the wave and dip of barley, feathering to a gentle July breeze. The lowland people descry herein the shadow of the forest

as they call it ; and the " Dartymorevolk," looking down upon them, are proud to have such a
long " tail to the moor."

For the line of the land is definite here, as
the boundary of a parish is. In many other
parts it is not so, and the moor slopes off into
farmland ; but here, like the fosse of an old
encampment, the scarp of the moor is manifest.
Over this, that well-fed stream, the Christow,
takes a rampant leap, abandoning craggy and
boggy cradle, desolate nurture, and rudiments
of granite, for a country of comparative ease,
where it learns the meaning of meadow. And
its passage, from rude into civilized life, occurs
in the garden of the " Captain." Brief is its
course, and quickly run ; for in the morass,
where it first draws breath, three other rivers
of wider fame arise, and go their several ways ;
and one of them, after twenty miles of crooked
increase round the North, quietly absorbs poor
Christow brook, and makes no gulp of acknowledgment. Without wasting one pebble in
calculation, or a single furrow upon forethought,
the merry brook hurries to whatever may befall
it, and never fails to babble of whatever comes
across it.

Now it happened that the vicar of the parish,

Mr. Short, was a "highly temperate" man, as all who love cold water are supposed to be; although they may love many other things therewith. No sooner had he seen Master Pugsley up the hill, with a strong shove to second old Teddy's motion, than he left those two to go in, and deliver the relics of their cargo, and their own excuses.

"Do'e come in now, and break it to the cappen," the carrier vainly pleaded to him; "do'e like a dear good minister."

"Tell your own lies, your own way," the parson answered pleasantly; "if I were there, I should have to contradict you."

"How partikkler you be—outzide of the pulpit!" said Pugsley with a sigh, yet a grin at his own wit.

Well seasoned to such little jokes, the Vicar looked at him seriously, so that the carrier felt sorry for his wit; and then, with a smile, Mr. Short went back to the place where he had left his coat. This was just over against the pile of pots, which had found the ground too hard, and had lost all tenure of it for ever. Looking at these, as he donned his coat, the parson said, "Ha! The newest, I believe, of that wonderful man's inventions! Let me take the liberty of looking at the fragments." This he soon accomplished to his heart's content, but failed to make head or tail of them, because he was not a born gardener. Then he took up a shord of one rounded side and went down to the river, with that for his cup. Not that he felt any thirst, although he had worked very hard—for a parson; but that a certain school of doctors had arisen, and said that every man, who wished to live, must take his cold pint every morning of his life. Some ten years later, every man, desirous to prolong himself and his family, was bound to take four gallons, shed outside him. And now he takes shivering claret inside.

For the nostrums of the moment Mr. Short cared little; but people had praised him, for liking now and then a draught of cold water; and this made him try to do it. With his slip of pantile, as he called it (in large ignorance of garden ware) he passed through a gap in the hedge of the lane, and walked down to the brook, and scooped up a little drink.

Assuring himself how delicious it was, he was going to pitch the shord into the stream, when he spied on its inner rim certain letters, invisible until the cloam was wetted.

" What a queer thing ! And how could it have been done ? " he thought, as he began to peer more closely; and then he made out the words—" Pole's patent." He tried it, several times, and he turned it several ways; but nothing else was to be made of it. And presently his own surprise surprised him, for what was there marvellous in the matter ? Nothing whatever ; but it was rather queer that the brand should be inside the pot (which must have required a convex mould) and the name not that of Mr. Arthur, although the design was entirely his, as Mr. Short knew, from having seen the drawings.

" What a blessing for me that I am not gifted with much curiosity ! " said the vicar to himself, as he turned the last corner of the lane, and sat down by the captain's gate, to wait till the carrier's job was done. " Nine out of ten of my brother clerks would have it on their conscience, to rout up this question. A mystery in one's own parish is a pest, when the man at the bottom of it comes to church. Otherwise one might wash one's hands. But this man is honest, and God-fearing, and a gentleman ; and the only one fit to smoke a pipe with in the parish ! "

Mr. Short sighed ; for he liked his fellow-men, and was partly cut off from them by his condition, or at least by his own view of it. Though many of the moorland pastors still looked after their flock, in a gregarious manner, not disdaining their assemblage at the public-house sometimes. " Our mysterious friend," he continued, as he gazed, " not only has a very large amount of taste, but also much strategic power. How well he has made his garden fit the stream, so that the stream seems to follow the garden! Grass in the proper place, beds in the proper place, and trees planted cleverly to drink the water, and flourish like the righteous man! But greatest device of all, and noblest, because of its pure simplicity, the safe-guard against morning calls, and the check to inquisitive ladies; for instance, Lady Touch-wood. How I should like to know that man's history! Hi, there, Pugsley! Give me a lift over. I can't jump, as I used to do."

A man's resemblance to a tree has been dis-covered, and beautifully descanted upon—from nethermost tail of tap-root, to uttermost twig, and split sky-leaf—by hundreds of admirable poets. But thoroughly as these have worked out the subject, they seem to have missed one most striking analogy. A man (like a tree)

can have no avail of comfort, unless there belongs to him the margin of a brook, to part
him from the brambles, and the ruffle, and the
jostle of the multitudinous thicket of the world.

"Lark's cot"—as Mr. Arthur's home was
called by the natives, and even by himself, at
last—was gifted with a truly desirable brook
—the Christow, as aforesaid. The cot stood
about a mile above the village, under a jagged
tor, known as "the beacon," and in a south-
eastern embrasure of the moor. This lonely,
quiet, and delightful spot looked as if it ought
to have no road to it, or at any rate none to go
any further. Upon its own merits indeed it
never would have earned or even claimed a
road: but it fell into the way of one, by a
"casual haxident," as Devonshire people term it.
For it happened, that one of the feeders of the
main Roman road, across the desert, helped itself
up the steep labour of the heights, by the
crooked balustrade of the Christow brook. This
lane, every now and then, cold-shouldered the
merriment of the brook, with a stiff dry hedge,
and feigned to have nothing to do with it; yet
times there were, and as much as a fortnight of
Sundays in a downright season, when lane and
brook made exchange of duty, as lightly as two

parsons do. And the public,—so faithful to variety it proves—was pleased in this case, as it is in the other; and after a while found a new charm, in recurring to its veteran and inveterate ruts.

But in moderate weather, and decent seasons, the Christow keeps to its natural bed, strewn with bright pebbles, and pillowed with rock. Through the garden of the captain, its glittering run is broken, by some little zig-zags of delay, and many laughing tumbles; at one of which, it does some work, by turning a wheel, when driven to it. And when the gardener's day is done, and the sun is gone to the western world, while the apple with uplifted, and the pear with pensive eye, stand forth of their dim leafage, in the rounding of the light—then down here, by the fluid steps, and twinkling passage of the stream, a bench is hung with clematis, and tented round with roses, for leisure, and the joy of rest, and bliss of admiration.

Now dwelling here, and seeing how the land was in his favour, the captain helped the hand of nature, to secure his quietude. The cliff on the west of his garden had offered possibility of descent, to ladies of clear head, and strong ankle. This bad temptation he soon removed, by a few charges of rock-powder; and then towards the north, where the ground was softer, he planted a brake of the large-flowered gorse, having thorns of stiff texture and admirable teeth. The bloom of this was brighter than the fairest maiden's tresses, even of the now most fashionable ochre; and the rustle of the wind, among the tufts, was softer than the sweetest silvery nonsense.

Thus he well established ramparts, solid and spinous, all about his rear; and then he had leisure to improve his front, and eastern flank towards the village. Nature had defended these, fairly and honestly enough, by sending a nice watercourse around them. Still there were lapses in the vigilance of the brook, where a lady, with her skirts up, might flip through, or even, with a downward run, spring over; and having much experience of the world, he knew how slow they were to hesitate, with curiosity behind them. So, with a powerful spade, and stout dredging-rake, he made good those weak places; and then looking round, with glad defiance, suddenly espied at his very threshold a traitorous inroad, a passage for the evil one. For here was a series of wicked stepping-stones, coming across a shallow width of water, as old

as the hills, and looking quite as steadfast.
Strictly heeding these, and probing vigorously
with a crowbar, he found one towards the
further side, which was loose in its socket, like
a well-worn tooth; and after a little operation,
he contrived to leave a fine gap in the series.
Curiosity on tiptoe might come thus far, but
without winged toes, or wading boots, was sure
of catching cold, if it came any further. Thus
a gentleman's wife, from a parish down below,
who kept the spy-glass of the neighbourhood, was obliged to stop there; and at once
pronounced him a vastly superior, and most
interesting man, but undoubtedly a noted
criminal.

CHAPTER V.

"How beautiful everything looks, and how large and early all your bloom is! People may talk about Torquay. But I was down there yesterday, and I find you a week in front of them. Well done, Christowell! Torquay has not a pear-bloom open yet, even in Morgan's garden. But perhaps you grow the earlier sorts."

Parson Short, and Captain Larks, were hearty friends by this time; for each of them loved the truthful staple, and kindly heart of the other. The clergyman had too much self-respect, to pry into the layman's history. He took him as he found him, a gentle, intelligent, peaceful, and orthodox ratepayer.

"The earliest fruit is not the first to bloom," the gardener answered, with his pruning-knife

at work; "or at any rate, not of necessity.
The later kind often is the first in bloom."

"Well, I never knew that. But I see the
reason. Slow fellows want a good start, as in
a race. I like to hear of little things, that I
have never noticed; for an apple and a pear are
pretty much the same to me. And that reminds
me of the thing I came to ask you. Yesterday
I rode down to Torquay, because the dog *Nous*
wanted exercise; and there, upon the pier, I
met an ancient friend, whom I value and admire
greatly. By the death of an uncle, he has
come into a large estate, on the west side of the
moor; and there he is going to improve the
garden. He has never had a chance of gardening much; but he loves it, almost as much as
you do, especially the fruit, and the vegetable
stuff. He knows next to nothing about it;
but that adds enormously to the enchantment.
He has heard of you, as a mighty man of fruit,
from nurserymen near Exeter. And instead
of burning, as he should have done, to come
and see me, the parson, all he seemed to care
about was to see you; you, the gardener, and
your garden!

"I ought to be obliged to him, even more
than I am," Mr. Arthur answered plainly.

" One of the many plagues of gardening is that the public regard it as a mere amusement, which is carried on, for them to stare at, like cricket on the village-green. The general idea of a garden is—a place to sit down in, and smoke pipes."

" And the right view of the subject too," replied Mr. Short, who understood his man, and how soon his petulance broke up into a smile. " My friend, I will take your hint. My pipe is ready. I will sit, and watch your labours, and learn much."

"That you will never do," the other answered, smiling at the turn of the mood upon him; " simply because it is not in you. From morning till night, you might think you were watching, and go away, not a twig the wiser, because you were not born for it; any more than I for Greek verbs, and pithy sermons. Why do I cut to this bud now? I have told you fifty times, but you cannot tell me now."

" Slash away all the buds," said Mr. Short, for fear of making a wrong hit at it; " so long as you know, and the bud understands it—but here comes the fairest bud of all, my little Rose-bud—how are you, my dear? And why does your father cut back to you? Is it because you grow in the right direction?"

"I have stopped growing long ago in every direction;" she answered, looking far away above the hat of Mr. Short; for her views of life were becoming large; and it liked her not to be called "my dear," even from the force of habit. And then she feared that she had gone too far, especially in looking such a height above him. So she blushed, in pure penitence,—and was almost ready to offer her father's friend a kiss, as used to be done of old, when she met him on the first morning of the holidays. But the vicar took no offence, and heeded not her communings, for he did not want to enter into young girls' minds.

"Now what would this child do, to express her gratitude"—he put it to her father with a nod of understanding; "supposing that I were to bring her a hero? A genuine hero, of valour and of chivalry, such a man as she has only dreamed of—or perhaps read about him, and got tired."

"I never get tired of reading of heroes; and how could I get tired of looking at them?"

"That is quite another pair of shoes, Miss Rose. My friend is not wonderful to look at, as the men seldom are, who have wrought great wonders. But you could not help liking and admiring him, because he does it to himself so little. And he will admire you, I can tell you. Coax your dear father to let me bring him."

"My poor little place, and my puny experiments," Mr. Arthur said, with that large humility, which marks the true gardener (as long as he is praised), "are always at the service of the lover of the craft, who is good enough to think, that I can teach him something. At the same time, it must be kindly borne in mind, that I am but a learner, and make no pretence to knowledge."

"To be sure, my dear sir. All allowance will be made. We cannot, for instance, expect you to be like the great Scotch gardener, at Lord Bicton's place."

"It would grieve me, and disgrace me, to be like that fellow. I would not let him come here, with his crooked-bladed knife, if he paid me £5 a day for it. Miserable numskull!"

"Even I should know better than to do what he does," cried Rose, running up to a fine pear-tree. "He nails the young wood of a wall-tree down the trunk, like this positively; and drives the great nails into the poor thing's breast!"

" Excellent idea ! " cried Mr. Short, laughing at the horror on the maiden's face. " So he makes the tree really self-supporting; and it feeds its young, like a pelican, out of its own breast."

" No; it feeds the nails, like that," she answered ; " the great rusty nails, and the dirty weeds, and snails ; and no nourishment for the poor fruit at all. Oh, Mr. Short, how very little you do know ! "

" How may I attain to such rare knowledge? If I only had the stuff in me, you might improve it. But alas, I have not the most raw material. But my old friend across the moor has got the making in him ; and he seems to see the principles, if he could only get the practice."

" So far as concerns my scraps of knowledge, and my humble premises," the owner answered, as he looked about him, with no other flourish than a clapping of his clips ; " they are wholly at the service of a friend of yours. It will give me great pleasure to see him, when he pleases. And if you will let me know the day, I will have my little drawbridge down."

" Now, I call that really kind of you ; because I know that you are pressed for time just now. And that made me enlist little Rosie on my side.

I will write at once to Colonel Westcombe; he will ride over to my early dinner, at which I shall be proud if you, and your dear child, will join us. Then we will have the old four-wheel out, and come up the hill all together."

"Oh, what a pleasure it will be! Papa, you had better not say 'No'; or you never shall hear the last of it. But what have you discovered so important in the brook? Is it a salmon? No, they can't get up here. It must be the otter once more. Mr. Short, oh do come with *Nous*, and your double-barrelled gun."

"It is not at all an easy thing to shoot an otter," said the parson, a dear lover of the rod and gun; "but if you have an otter here, he will harry your trout dreadfully. The only way to get a shot is to lie hid for hours. *Nous* would do more harm than good, freely as he takes the water. But, Arthur, you understand all that. I am sure that you are an old sportsman."

"I used to be fond of the gun," said his host; "but I never shoot now; and shall never shoot again."

Mr. Short was surprised at the tone of his voice, and the change in his face, and manner. What was become of his frank complacence, and light smile at his own conceit, and glances of fatherly pride at his Rose?   Instead of all that he looked troubled, and perplexed, and preparing to contend with some new grief.   Even his lively child saw this; though as yet she had not learned to study a face, whose only expression for her was love.

"I fear that I have vexed you," the clergyman said kindly; "by striving to draw you from your good and quiet habits.   I can well understand your dislike to be disturbed, such as I very often have myself.   Leave it to me to settle with Colonel Westcombe.   I can easily do it, without offending him.   The fault has been wholly my own, for not considering.   I hope that you will pardon me; and I am sure that Westcombe will; for he is one of the noblest-hearted fellows living."

"That he is.   Right well I know it," Mr. Arthur answered, with more warmth than prudence.   "But alas, what a number of my pots are broken!   Let us go in.   The sun is droughty.   We have hit upon a most prime blend of cider; but I dare not bottle any, till I have your *imprimatur*."

"You shall have the full benefit of my judgment," the parson answered briskly; "after the tug of the morning, I deserve even better than Christow water. My acquaintance with fruit is chiefly liquid, in spite of all your lectures. Miss Rose, answer me one question, if you can ; and young ladies now-a-days are taught all paradoxes. Why should milk become solid, and apples liquid, by the self-same process of thumping ?"

" Because, because—because I don't know. And can you explain to me, Mr. Short, how a man can be beaten black, and blue ? If he is black, he can never be blue."

" Nothing can be simpler. At first he is black ; and as he begins to get better he turns blue."

Such nonsense they were talking, not of their own folly, but simply to carry off the awkward time, as they followed Captain Larks to the cottage. He turned round, now and then, to seem to heed them ; but they knew, better than himself perhaps, that his mind was far away, and that his cheerfulness was gone. Then he roused up his spirits, to discharge fair duties as a host, at which he was always good, with the very few whom he received as guests. His graceful young daughter, with her hat thrown off, and clusters of nut-brown hair tied back, flitted across the bars of sunshine chequered by some Banksian sprays, while she spread upon the table shadow, and still better, substance of the things that nourish life. Bread, that is to say, and butter (beaded as with meadow dew); honeycomb, gladdened with the moorland scent, and the thick-set mettle of a home-fed ham, where fat and lean played into one another sweetly—like moonlight among roses. In the thick of temptation reposed Cos-lettuce—cold and crisp, and beautiful, and justly divided by a thin, sharp knife, showing follicle, frill, and crimp broidery of gold, in and out of cells, and fronds, and filigree of carved ivory. Neither were the fluid creatures absent; cider was there, like an amber fountain springing into beads of pearl, and bright ale, comrade of the labours of mankind; and, for the weaker vessels, water. Not yet was vapid claret shed, like vinegar on the English rock.

Distributing good supply, and partaking fairly to commend it, the host began to regard the world, with larger benevolence, and hope. He looked at his child, who was doing her best to smile away sudden disturbance, and to set their visitor at his ease; and then he looked at this pleasant friend, who had shown such good breeding, and submission to his mood. And with that, Mr. Arthur was fain to confess, that he had allowed himself to be surprised out of his usual respect for others.

The vicar, (although a testy man, with strangers, or with upstarts,) not only did not show, but did not even feel resentment now. He had faith in his friend, that there must be sound reason for the refusal of his request; and he fully expected some explanation, perhaps when Rose should be out of the way. So he thoroughly enjoyed the simple fare, and resolved to enrage his cook, Mrs. Aggett, by a fulsome description of the captain's ham. For this he deserved to have his banquet interrupted, and so it was very speedily.

"Well, I do declare," cried the quick-eyed Rose, as she helped him to some honey for the crown of his repast, "the very queerest figure that you can imagine is trying to get across our steps!"

"Ungrateful damsel!" Mr. Short replied, as he went to the bud-covered lattice. "Have you no sense of a most distinguished honour? It is the mighty Solomon, and he bears a letter."

"Surely you don't mean Betty Cork's boy,

who went about for Doctor Perperaps? The one that rose into the ‘loftier spear?’”

“To be sure; Lady Touchwood’s page he is. And she so arrays him, that our wag, the cobbler’s boy, who used to call him ‘Solomon Senna,’ now has dubbed him ‘Solomon’s Glory.’”

“Glorious he may be,” said Rose; “but he seems in a very sad fright at present; and he cannot take my jump. Father, dear, shall I go, and ask him what he wants?”

“After all, the honour is not for you, but my humble self,” interposed Mr. Short. “He is screaming at the top of his voice ‘Passon Shart.’ Don’t think of letting down the draw-bridge. I will make him walk through, just to spoil his grand livery.”

“Oh, if you are not afraid of ‘my lady,’ do make him walk through the water, while I see him.”

“Rose, you are too mischievous,” said Mr. Arthur, getting up. “I will go and take the boy’s message myself. We must not carry things too far.”

In a minute or two, he returned with a letter, sealed with a formidable coat of arms, and addressed to “The Revd. Tom Short, Christo-well Vicarage. *Important.*”

" Plague upon the woman ! " cried the reverend gentleman ; " she wants me on the instant, about something most momentous ! And Mrs. Aggett has been stupe enough to send the boy on here. It is nothing but one of her little tempers. However, I must go home, and ride away at once, though my horse is entitled to a good day in stable."

" I wanted to show you a whole quantity of things," replied his host with unfeigned disappointment ; for the bloom of the pleasure of good work fades, when nobody comes to admire it. " It is more than a fortnight since you were here ; and a fortnight of April is as much as a month, at almost any other time. And if you care little for fruit, you love flowers."

" The rose, the rose, the rose for me ! " Mr. Short exclaimed, with a smile at the blushing specimen before him. " I shall write you the song of the rose some day. I know a little Rose, who considers me a nightingale. Even so, I must fly immediately. May I let down the planch for myself, good host ? "

They would not hear of this, but bore him company down the winding walk ; where the pear-tree was clustering its petal'd cups of snow, and the apple beginning, in the slant sunshine, to unravel the down of its bossy green truss. Then the gardener himself let down his "planch," over the wavering glitter of the brook ; and crossing the meadow, where Mopsy the cow lived, they came to the private door into the lane. Here Christowell shone, in the haze of spring below them, and the hoary old church, beyond the flash of hasty waters, looked holy, and peaceful, as the tombs around it.

"Be sure that you come again soon," cried Rose, running lightly back to the lane, while her father was going home across the mead. "Please to come to-morrow, if you possibly can, and tell us every syllable about that Lady Touchwood ; she puzzles me so dreadfully, Mr. Short !"

"Lady Touchwood will say, when she hears where I have been, 'Tell me every syllable about that Miss Arthur ; she is such a puzzle to me, Mr. Short !'"

No sooner had he spoken than he deeply regretted his stupid little slip of tongue ; because he saw that he had given pain. Rose made no answer, but coloured deeply, and turned away with a curtsey ; then, rejoining her father, she clung closely to his arm.

"Poor dear !" thought the vicar, who loved

his light-hearted, and sweet parishioner, pastor-ally, "I heartily trust, that I am altogether wrong. But, if I know anything of the world, that pretty girl, and good girl, has a troublous time before her."

CHAPTER VI.

A TINGLE AND A TANGLE.

TOUCHWOOD PARK, as the owners loved to call it, differed from Lark's Cot, almost as much as Sir Joseph Touchwood from " Captain Larks." Brilliance without shade, but striped, and barred with brighter brilliance, and slashed across with all bold hues (in diaper pattern, glittering like a newly varnished oil-cloth) with stucco pilasters to relieve it (but all too shallow to help themselves, or carry their white perukes of pie-crust), and topped with a stuck-up roof of tile, and puckered things called " minarets," but more like stable-lanterns —the gazer found solace in shutting both eyes, and hoping that the money had done good elsewhere.

" Winderful to my maind, winderful they arktexts be!" said John Sage, of Christowell, to his wife. " Blest if they han't diskivered a plan, to make tower of Babel, out of Noah's rainbow!"

"What odds to thee?" replied his good wife sharply; "our Bill hath drawed his ladder wages, riglar, every Zatterday."

Truly, it made small difference to the quiet folk of Christowell, whether the mansion were tall or short, dazzling or soothing to the eye; because it was out of their parish—which marks a broad line in all matters of feeling—and also, because it was out of their sight, till they mounted a gristly and scraggy bone of hill. Some of them looked upon this as a great denial, and grumbled, at going so far, to see the big house on a Sunday. But most people said it was wisely ordained, lest the liver'd young men should come courting their daughters, and drive up the price of beer at the *Horse-shoes*.

Sir Joseph Touchwood had a right to please himself; as indeed he always did, having vast self-complacence, which was justified by his success in life. Beginning his career, as a boy of all work, he had made his way into a little grocer's shop at Stonehouse, and so into the Pursers' rooms, and thence into Admiralty contracts, lucrative, and elastic. He cheated as little as he could help, until he could do it, on a worthy scale, and in superior company.

Rising thus, he was enabled, by-and-by, to be the superior company himself, to reward those who helped him, and make it more expedient, to shake the head, than to wag the tongue about him. And little as he cared for the shadow, or even the sparkle of his object, while he grasped the substance, the showy part also was rendered to him, by a pleasing and natural incident.

Lord Wellington's men having worn out their shoes, by constant pursuit of the enemy, our Government took measures to prepare to shoe them, by the time they had learned to march barefoot. Joseph Touchwood got the contract; his beef had been found of such durable texture, that the hides, in all reason, must last for ever. The order was placed in Northampton; the shoes were made in a jiffy, and came to Plymouth, two-and-twenty thousand of them, all of a size, not in pairs, but polygamous; being shaped so admirably, as to fit either human foot alike. They passed a triumphant examination, and were happily shipped to a Spanish port, which fell into the hands of Marshal Soult, on the very day of their arrival.

That great commander rejoiced exceedingly; for his men were bare-footed, from running away; and he rigged out eleven thousand Gallic heroes, in captured British leather—or the like. On the very next day, a great battle came off, and the right side won it,—that is to say, ours. Then every Frenchman (shot, lanced, or taken prisoner) was proved to be as lame as a cock on a glassed wall; and although no allowance was made for that drawback, the hand of Providence was discovered in it. It was useless for Touchwood to deny that he had foreseen this result, and produced, at great outlay, a patriotic stratagem. In a word, with no more waste of time, than was needful for the British Cabinet to conceive, ponder, and deliver a large budget of jokes at the Frenchman's expense, of his vain attempt to fill British leather, and getting into the wrong pair of shoes, etc.—amid public applause, they made the contractor a baronet, instead of paying him.

Sir Joseph would liefer have received the money; for the shoes stood him fairly in 9*d.* a-piece; and he counted for a further loss his non-gain of three shillings, upon every one of them. He had no honest ground for complaint however, having run a good cargo of French goods homeward, as well as established a permanent basis for supplying the French, through the rest of that campaign, with slop-flannel trousers, as blue as their legs.

Sir Joseph worked harder than ever, although universally respected by this time. And though he cared little for empty honour, he loved fame, when it led to business. Lady Touchwood began to think more of his opinion, and allowed him no longer to be called, " our Joe." He flourished exceedingly ; but stuck to business still, and left all the decorative part to her. This lady was an admirable wife, and mother, kind, warm-hearted, full of interest in things that were no concern of hers, an excellent adviser, when not consulted, as good to the poor as they would let her be, vigilant in her own household, and resolute in having her own way always. The most captious of critics could find no fault in her, except that she was obstinate, imperious, narrow-minded, and ridiculously passionate, when " put out." And a very little thing was enough to put her out; though she always believed it to be monstrous.

" Now I call it very good of you, to come to me so promptly ; " she exclaimed, holding out both hands to Mr. Short. " I always like people to do that, so much. Never mind anything. Do sit down."

Mr. Short bowed pleasantly, but made no pretty speech; though the ladies still expected such politeness from the gentlemen. For he knew that this lady would only cut short his oration.

"I am the most persecuted person in the world," she continued, glancing sadly at a statuette of Dido; "no, she was not to be compared to me, and she did burn the villain who betrayed her!"

"Sir Joseph?" inquired Mr. Short with some surprise, but too wary to correct the lady's memory of the Æneid.

"Sir Joseph! How can you be so exceedingly provoking? Sir Joseph is a model; and besides that, he knows better. It is my daughter, Julia."

"I am grieved indeed," Mr. Short said softly, and dropping his eyes, lest they should gleam with any levity. "The young lady promised to behave so well; and she seemed so truly sorry, so affectionate, and dutiful, after having shown a little—temper perhaps, on Monday."

"Then, you shall hear how she has kept her promise. This morning, without provocation or excuse, she packed up all her property, and she left my house!"

"Surely, there must have been something more than usual?"

"Not at all. You shall judge for yourself. She is constantly pretending to have judgments of her own, and to use what she calls her reasoning powers. No good ever comes of such a thing as that. But she is at liberty to do it, when she pleases; so long as she only agrees with me. But to argue against her own mother, Mr. Short!"

"Lady Touchwood, I agree with you, that it is wrong. But of course, with your superior intellect, you convinced her of her error."

"That I did thoroughly. I boxed her ears; until they were as red as the things they make sauce of. Oh, it was such a satisfaction to me!"

Mr. Short stared a little, though he knew the lady's temper. Then he thought of the haughty tall Julia, whom he admired with a distant fervency. Julia, with her pretty ears as red as ripe tomatoes!

"I hurt my poor hands shockingly, with her nasty brilliants. It was too bad of her." Lady Touchwood exhibited her dimpled, but vigorous palms, with pink lines on them. "She went to bed, as I thought, in a chastened spirit; and I told her to pray for a better frame of mind. But instead of that, she has done what I tell you."

"But you know where she is? You have ascertained that, otherwise you would be in great tribulation. Is she gone to her father, at Plymouth?"

"Not she indeed. Sir Joseph has too much high principle, to encourage her; though he would, no doubt, if he dared; because she can do exactly as she likes with him."

"Then perhaps, to her aunt at Ivybridge? I am sure that you know; or you would be more sorry for what you have done, Lady Touchwood."

"I do the right thing, and I defy the consequence. But I know where the hussy is well enough. I ought to have taken her purse away. She has hired a post-chaise, and driven off forsooth, in noble state, to Westcombe Hall."

"To Colonel Westcombe's place! I had not the least idea, even that you knew him. I have spoken of him, and you made no sign." Mr. Short looked surprised, for he was thinking— "Well, you can hold your tongue, when you please, as well as people of better temper."

"Oh dear yes," replied Lady Touchwood, as if she were surprised at his surprise; "we have known Colonel Westcombe, for years and years, in fact he is Julia's godfather, and immensely proud she is of him. But circumstances—well you know, there was no particular reason why one should go running after him, until he came into that large property; and that, as you must be aware, was not at all expected."

"It is an honour to any one, to know Colonel Westcombe. Land, or no land, rich, or poor, no circumstances make any difference in his value."

"I dare say. But still, you know, it adds to his charms, to be in a good position. Sir Joseph was thinking of inviting him to dinner; but I must see first, how he behaves about my daughter. If he encourages poor Julia in her headstrong violence, and evil tempers, he shall never sit down in this house, Mr. Short."

"Whatever he does will be right, Lady Touchwood, whatever your opinion may be about it. And now, though I am not the clergyman of your parish, you have given me the right to speak, by sending for me. And setting aside all the folly of your conduct, I must tell you, that it is very wrong."

Mr. Short spoke strongly; for he feared no one, and cared very little for the temper of any woman, except his own Mrs. Aggett. He expected to be shown to the door, with much despatch. But instead of that, his hostess bore meekly with him, and even seemed to listen with attention. For she knew in her heart, that she had gone a little too far, peradventure, and she respected the established church, whenever she was not furious. In her youth, she had been a quiet, gentle-looking person, with large blue eyes, and a plump round face, and delicate complexion. But, even then, the doubling of the chin, the bold cut of nostril, and fulness of the eyelid, showed that mischief might come out, and patience not strike root in age.

"Is your homily over?" she inquired with a smile, which saved her words from rudeness; for like many other quick-tempered persons, she had a very pretty smile, to put her in the right. "You are famous for very short sermons, with a very great deal in them. How I wish you were our vicar here, instead of Mr. Barker! He always goes on, for three quarters of an hour."

"Barker is a very sound and excellent divine. Many of my people long for him. I always get him over, for collection-Sundays. He draws half-a-crown, where I draw a shilling. My farmers say, ' short time makes short wages.' But, what have you sent for me to do, about your fair deserter?"

" To advise me, Mr. Short; because you are so clever. People are so liable to misunderstand me. They never make allowance for the trials I encounter. Sir Joseph is all the week long at his office ; and I have to go through every hardship by myself. Even if he were here, this moment, I could not allow him to interfere; because he is so one-sided. He looks upon Julia, as a perfect angel, because she understands his snuff so well. She gets on her father's blind side so cleverly, the crafty young time-server!"

" But your son, Lady Touchwood—your admirable son ? "

" Dicky is a model of every known virtue ; but he spends all his time, with the rat-catcher's dogs. At this time of year, it is most important to get the rats thinned off, you know. And, besides that, he takes such extraordinary views, that he goes against me very often. I have felt it my duty, to have this matter kept from him, for fear of his taking it, in an unbecoming manner."

"Which means, in plain English, that he would side with his sister. It was very good of her, to go away, without involving him. But something must be done, and done at once, if possible. You have not allowed the servants to discover, I suppose, the cause of this sudden departure."

"Their opinions are nothing whatever to me. If they form nasty ones, I discharge them. But Julia has much more dignity, I should hope, than to whine, about what she has brought upon herself. She could not help feeling, that she brought it on herself."

"Very well, then," replied Mr. Short, to avoid that difficult subject, "we may treat the matter, as a simple visit of the young lady to her dear godfather. The servants, and the stable-men, may be wroth, at being dispensed with, or endeavour to be so; but upon the whole, the less they have to do, the more thoroughly they enjoy it. You, on the other hand, show no anxiety, but leave the fair fugitive to her own devices. She, in her exile, begins to pine for her birds, and her books, her flowers, her piano, and her pet dog, Elfie."

"No, not Elfie. She has taken that wretch with her. You may trust her, never to stir a

yard, without darling Elfie. She may pine, as
you say, if she is capable of it ; but surely, the
first thing she should pine for, is her own good
mother."

" So she will, and very painfully indeed. And
the end of it is, that she writes a touching letter,
and comes home, with a wholesome knowledge,
that the ears must expiate the tongue's
offences."

" You know nothing at all about her," Lady
Touchwood answered, with a mother's smile.
" What does a bachelor know of women ? They
calculate on them, from their own reason. For
instance, do you think, that I could wait a
month, with my daughter in the hands of other
people, and learning all sorts of tricks, against
her own mother ? I can be very patient, and
most long-suffering, when I am convinced that
my trials require it. But as for sitting down
like this, and thinking, and hoping for people to
be reasonable, your own sense must show you
that I never, never could put up with it. Surely
you must have some wiser plan than that ! "

" I will tell you then, what I will do, if you
think fit.   I will call upon my old friend,
Colonel Westcombe, if you wish me to do so,
and see Miss Touchwood."

" Not as if you came from me, of course. Julia would get the upper hand directly. But why not go to-day, Mr. Short? The days are getting nice and long, and it is not very far."

" Twelve good miles, as the crow flies," said her visitor, thinking to himself that she deserved some brisk anxiety; " and the crow would have many steep hills, to fly over. My horse took me forty miles yesterday, and more. And if I went now, it would look as if you were devoured with regret, and penitence; and that would be below your dignity. To-morrow, I have an engagement of importance. But, unless you send to stop me, I shall make a point of being there in good time, on Saturday morning. You will see her on Saturday, by dinner-time; it takes a little time, to get over such things."

" It ought to be sooner, but it must not be later. Remember that Sir Joseph will be home that evening; and if he should not have done well, that week, he might make a whole string of troublesome inquiries. You must not think me selfish. That is the last thing to be said of me. But I like people to be considerate to me, and amiable, and sweet-tempered. And I have a good right to expect it, Mr. Short, for I am always so to others—when they let me."

"Ah, yes, I see. But how fond you are of self-examination, Lady Touchwood! Is it because you find the result so favourable?"

"I am never put out, by sarcastic speeches; because I don't understand them. I hope you will come, and dine with us on Sunday, if that dreadful Mrs. Aggett will allow you."

The vicar was never ashamed to say, that he heartily loved a good dinner. How many a parson has got his living, by knowing what good living is? Wherefore are college kitchens far more glorious than the lecture-rooms, and why does the buttery excel the chapel? Therefore Mr. Short said yes, with a very cheerful countenance; and observed with tender resignation, as he rode home through the park, that the fattest of the bucks was absent.

CHAPTER VII.

As with many species of monœcious plants, so with some families of human kind, the female flower transcends the male, in beauty, size, and dignity. In all these points, Sir Joseph Touchwood, and Richard, his only son, fell far below the mark of the ladies they belonged to. The father, and founder, was an admirable man, when regarded from a national, that is to say, from a business point of view. He had never been known, except by himself, to miss a chance of getting on; and from day to day, he became more honest, as his character increased. Plymouth began to respect him deeply, as she found his vigour enlarge her trade, and some Radical deputations begged him to go up to Parliament. However, he had too much sense for that; and managed to get out of it, without offence to any one. But several of his school-fellows, who had not got on so well, thoroughly agreed with one another, that "Sandy Joe" (as they still called him) was making a fool of himself, in building, over there by Dartmoor, that popinjay, pack-of-cards, peep-show thing, like the Lord Mayor's coach in London; and, unless they were very much mistaken, such a stuck-up lot would come down headlong. Sir Joseph, as soon as he heard of these sentiments, proved the largeness of his mind, by inviting all the critics to his great house-warming; and the few of them who went were so well treated, that they put down all the rest, who had no coats to go in.

A man who succeeds, with the hardest thing of all, and the highest in his opinion, that is to say, the money, is apt to believe that he can have his own way—if he chooses to assert it—in the lesser matters of life, such as family love, and respect, and the character of his children. The great contractor, perceiving that his son had no special turn for business, resolved to give him a fine education, and harness him afterwards, if needful. He sent him to a private school, and thence to Cambridge, and was proud to hear him called "the Cantab." The youth learned little, but was not dissatisfied, either with himself, or the world around him. For everybody looked upon him, as a pleasant fellow, free-handed, careless, and good-natured in his way, talkative, full of small adventures of his own, and not disagreeably truthful. He was never long without some mighty hero, whom he worshipped, for strength, or ability, or knowledge of the world, and who could have done better whatever was done well, and with less than a quarter of the trouble. Though indolent enough of mind, he was very restless bodily, and would keep the whole house upon the fidget, unless he got his daily exercise. And now, as he was missing his term at Cambridge, and no field-sports were toward, his mother considered it a special grace of Providence, in favour of her Dicky, that Dartmoor was invaded by a mighty host of rats. For, if there was anything that Dicky Touchwood thoroughly enjoyed, it was a good rat-hunt.

Now the fact that every one, high or low, who possessed the pleasure of his acquaintance—and one need not be very high to do that—called him without hesitation, "Dicky Touchwood," is as clear a proof as can be given, of his easy, careless style. His mother, and sister, had bravely striven, at the dates of his breeching, and then of his horsing, and then of his having

a tail thrown over, to redeem him from a Dicky,
into Richard, Dick, or Richie, or even the old-
fared Dickon. At each of these epochs, their
struggle was vain; but they rallied for a final
stand, upon the breastwork of his matriculation.
For many a mile, and league around them, none,
but some half a score of parsons, knew the
meaning of that mighty word; and possibly it
might have triumphed over nature, if the latter
had not ignobly adopted the *argumentum ad
hominem.* For the Cantab, upon his return, as
arranged by his mother. in full academical
plight, as he leaped from the chariot of the
Park, in the presence of the whole population,
upset the entire effect, by shouting—"Three
cheers, for Dicky Touchwood!"

His only sister, Julia, was of a very different
order. Tall, and handsome, and resolute, and
straight-forward, she kept her own place, and
followed her own liking. She reigned over her
father, when he was at home, and was fairly
reducing her mother to subjection, in spite of
some violent outbreaks. The latest of these
had filled her with amazement, even more than
with indignation; until she perceived, being
very clear-sighted, that it was a last despairing
effort, to cast off the tightening yoke. With

skilful management on her part, it would prove the final clenching of the link. Dicky was a far more uncertain subject, for there was not substance enough in him to bind.

The sportive Dicky made few inquiries, as to the reason of his sister's absence. When she was gone, he could have his own way, without let, or hindrance, until something disagreed with his mother. For he was her darling, her pet, and her idol, and he alone of mortals might ever contradict her. So now, he resolved to make the most of this fine opportunity, and be master, so far as he cared to be, which was chiefly in matters of sport, and of feeding. Ordering the household right and left, that very afternoon he sent for three rat-catchers, and commanded them to sink their feuds, till Sunday, and be ready for him at the Park-gate, the next morning, with every dog, and ferret, they could hear of, together with their shovels, wire-cages, knobsticks, and all the other items of their interesting gear. With the prospect of a guinea, and the certainty of beer, they were punctual as the sun, at ten o'clock; and a motley host of bipeds, quadrupeds, and tripods—for some of the dogs had only three feet left—set forth gallantly, to invade the rats of Dartmoor.

Meanwhile, on this same Friday morning, Mr. Arthur (generally known as " Captain Larks ") was busy with a lot of little vines in pots, which were crying out for more room, and more nurture. He had brought them, from his span-roof forcing-house, to a little glazed building of his own construction, snugly ensconced beneath the cliff. And here, with half a hundred of his new patent pots, he was craftily preparing a delicious compost, of mealy sod, mellow manure, and spicy bone-dust, enough to make the little mouths of dainty creatures water. At this he worked hard, without sparing his hands, pulling asunder the fibrous clods, but not reducing them to siftage, nipping in twain every wireworm, and grub, carefully distributing the sweet-stuff from the linhay, and the benefit of happy bones, that should never ache again, and lightly, with his open fingers, carding up the mixture; until the whole was sleek, and fragrant, with the vital gifts of earth.

None but a very gruff fellow, unworthy to love, or be loved by, nature, can minister thus to his little dependants, without ministering also to his own cares. Captain Larks was down-hearted, and perplexed, and quavery, when he drew his hand to do this work; but courage came to him, and the love of life, and the golden touch of hope, as he went on. The interest in other things beyond himself grew bright and gladsome, as he worked for good; and without thinking of it, he began to whistle the old English tune, "We won't give up." Last night he had said to himself, "I must give up. Fate is too much for me, and all things go against me. I must fly from this refuge of many quiet years, and of pet things, the fruit of my own work. I must fly somewhere else, and begin once more, with the loss of all the little relics of my money, and rheumatism settling in my left shoulder-blade. And, worst of all, with darling Rose astray, and quite bewildered."

But now, he was hoping for the best, and well believing that fear had made too much of his imaginary trouble. The day was fine, and the sunshine brisk, enlivening mankind, and especially those, who live among the offspring of the sun. The soft spring air, afloat with sunbeams, brought the blue distance of the heavens to the earth; and the white blossoms shone upon it, as if they saw it. The gardener, as he plied his work, was breathing sweet contentment, for his heart drank in the beauty; and, better still, at every breath, he felt that fruit was setting.

."Father, how glad I am, to see you look like your old self again!" cried Rose, coming in from the grass-walk. "Mr. Short is wonderfully good and kind; but I should simply hate him, if he were to begin to disturb your mind. You never ate as much as my thumb for supper; and you couldn't look worse, if I ran away from you."

"I scarcely know, how much your thumb eats for supper," her father replied, as his pleasure increased, with gazing at her bright, and affectionate face; "but, if it has not over-eaten itself, I would beg some help from it, with the ball of this vine."

"Now, if you don't know, papa, you ought to know," she said in a low voice, as they worked together; "and you ought to be punished, for not knowing well, that I am come to years of full discretion."

"It is a fine thing, to have a good opinion of oneself. There, you have proved your words, by snapping this root-fibre!"

Although he spoke thus, he was thinking to himself—"this daughter of mine is discreet, beyond her years. How she would enjoy her youth, if it were the same as other girls have ! And how beautiful she is, the pretty darling ! ”

As for that he was right beyond all doubt; though a father's pride goes astray sometimes, from cleaving, over-fondly, to the grooves of love. A very sweet face has its sweetness trebled, when tender doubt, and a light shade of anxiety, soften the bloom of the cheeks, and deepen the lustre of inquiring eyes. Rose Arthur (with the sun-gleam on her hair, and the pure white forehead touched with thought, and the delicate oval of the face enhanced by the suppliant curve of neck) was not only charming to look at, but also bewitching to think of afterwards.

“ How can I have at all a good opinion of myself,” she asked her father, with some twinkle of a tear, “ when nobody considers me of any use at all ? ”

“ What a bare-faced bit of fishing for a compliment ! Can I ever do anything, without you now ? And when have I failed to praise you, up to your deserts ? ”

“ I don't mean such trumpery things as potting—or at least they are not at all trumpery, I know—but what I mean is great things, about people's lives, and reasons for doing things, and not telling other people."

"My darling," said her father, without displeasure, for he saw that she was trembling at her own audacity, "I will not pretend to misunderstand you; neither have I any right to blame you. You want to know, why I live a different life from other people, whom you know; why I am so reserved, and lonely, and keep you shut up in this dull place."

"Father, I never had such an idea. The place is quite good enough for me, I should hope, if it is good enough for you. And, as for being lonely, what more can I want, than to have you, and help you, and try to be half as good to you, as you are to me?"

"Well, my little Rosy one, that is all very fine in theory. The practice, however, goes otherwise; or why are you asking questions now?"

"I never would have said a word, dear father, except that I cannot bear to see you vexed. It does not matter about myself; but when it comes to you, it is dreadful."

"But suppose, my pet, that it is only for you, that I care much about anything. Suppose that, for reasons which are not my own to tell, I am bound to keep my darling child from the roughness of the world; and can do it only, by keeping outside of the world, altogether. If that were so, you would have faith enough, to believe that I acted for the best, and love enough not to increase my cares, by questions which I cannot answer."

"Oh, father, I wish that I had bitten out my tongue, before I asked a single question. I will never be so cruel, and undutiful, again. But you will forgive me, for this once?"

"Rosy, I am very glad you did ask. It will make things happier between us, on the whole. You must have thought, a thousand times, that there was something odd about us. It is better to make up your mind to that, than to live in a doubtful suspicion of it. In the course of time, you will know the whole. But I fear that it will not be, while I live."

"Then I hope that it will never be, in this world, father. Whatever should I do without you? It is too dreadful!"

"There now, my darling, let us talk no more about it," said the father, with his child's tears on his cheeks; "we have got a lot of work to do; and let us give our minds to it. After all, there are millions of people in the world, not a thousandth part so happy as you, and I, may be, while we have one another's love to help us."

"I should like to see anybody impudent enough, to be happier than I am, all day long. I have never known an atom of unhappiness, in my life."

She gave a little sob, to prove her words, and caught her breath quickly, at such a mistake. Then she tossed up a heavy pot, and turned her sleeves up, to show what energetic arms she had.

"How they have grown in the night! Look at this!" she exclaimed, with a smile, that was full of delight. "Father, there is nothing, in all the world, more lovely than a baby vine, just when it begins to understand things, and offer its innocent hands to us. Look, for one moment, at this little darling; now, doesn't it seem to be toddling to me, with its tiny hands spread out? Papa, I am sure, there is nothing in the world half so beautiful as gardener's work. What are jewellers, or watchmakers, or ivory-carvers, or even painters, to compare with a genuine gardener? The things that they handle are dead, and artificial, and cannot know the meaning of the treatment they receive. But our work is living, and natural, and knows us, and adapts itself to follow our desires, and please us; and has its own tempers, and moods, and feelings, exactly the same as we have. For people to talk about 'sensitive plants' does seem to be such sad nonsense, when every plant that lives is sensitive. You are very busy; but just spare time, to look at this holly-leafed baby vine, with every tiny point cut like a prickle, yet much too tender and good to prick me. It follows every motion of my hand; it crisps its little veinings up, whenever I come near it; and it feels, in every fibre, that I am looking at it."

"It is in my power to swallow tales of gigantic bulk," Mr. Arthur replied, and then opened his mouth, to show its noble capacity; "especially, when they come from you, my dear. Nevertheless, after watching my vines for many years, I have never had the luck to receive such reciprocity. Please to show me, the next time you see them looking at you."

"As if I would be guilty of such treachery, papa! They know that I am foolish, and they like me for it. But you are much too wise for them, and scare them of their confidence. Stop a moment; did you hear that noise again? There has been such a noise, going on around the beacon. The glass has prevented you from hearing it, I suppose. I meant to have told you, till we spoke of something else. There seems to be a quantity of men, and dogs, up there, shouting, and barking, and screaming out, and making the greatest uproar."

"Whatever it is, I would strongly recommend them, to keep it outside of my premises. Halloa!"

Well indeed might he thus exclaim. A dark bulk fell upon the glittering roof; at the crash a shower of flashing splinters flew, like a bursting firework, and a human form tumbled in, all doubled up, and rolled upon a newly-potted platoon of those sensitive vinelets.

"Oh, he must be killed!" cried Rose, running up to him. "The poor unfortunate little boy! I have got his head up on a pot. Father, hold him up, till I get the water."

Rose herself was bleeding sadly, from the arrowy sleet of glass; but without two thoughts, she was off, and came back, with a long-spouted can, and put a copper spreader on it.

"No," said her father, as she held up the can, to water this gentleman freely; "not a drop of water. I have seen much bloodshed. Water would be wrong, in a case like this. Leave him to me. Run for bandages quickly; and send Moggy off, the short way to the village, quick foot, for Dr. Perperaps."

Rose was off, like a deer; and the gardener began, after drawing out one or two splinters of glass, and placing the youth in a better position, to close the worst cuts, with cotton wool (which he always kept in the greenhouse) tightly bound with broad strips of bast. Then he soaked the wool with cold water; and the patient gave a long gasp, and began to look about him.

"Not dead yet, my boys!" He tried to shout, but only muttered; "At him again, Tiger, at him again! Get him by the scruff, Bob; don't be an idiot. Hurrah, well done, Peppercorns!"

"Hold your tongue, sir, and shut your eyes," Mr. Arthur broke in, with his deepest tone; and the youth stared at him, and obeyed his voice, after putting up his lips, as if he longed to whistle. And while his mind went wandering, into wonder, and distant dimness, a little dog, with all his wits about him, came in at the door; and, making obeisance with a tremulous tail, asked courteous leave to sniff at him. Mr. Arthur, being fond of dogs, said, " Yes;" and before this dog could have satisfied his mind, two more came in, to help him. But the first dog, being of a kingly order, signified to them that they were not wanted; and when they retired at his growl, he joined them, and the three held council. As sagely as any three M.D.'s they conducted their consultation, with their ears upon the curl, and their tails upon the wag, so far as men had spared them. But suddenly all three stumps fell flat, and quivered with humility; for, lo! there stood their worshipful masters, puffing, and blowing, and inclined to swear, at having only two legs each, to bring them down the wall of crag.

"Cappen Larks, be 'un killed?" they cried, all scared to go into the greenhouse. "The young Squire Dicky, oh lor, oh lor; and all the vault to be laid on us! Back there with 'e, every one o' you chaps! Us'll lash the legs of any chaps, as trieth it. These be Cappen's own privy grounds, and no blackguards admitted in."

"Be off every one of you," the owner shouted, with a smile, which went against his words; "or in two minutes, you will be prosecuted, with the utmost rigour of the law."

"Cappen Larks, don't ye be so haish, for to deny us a zaight o' the poor Master Dicky.

There never wor a better one, to work a rat out; and if a' be killed, us 'll niver hunt again."

"My good fellows, he is not killed, and he won't be, if you will get out of the way. But I won't answer for it, if you come plaguing here. Be off, if you care for his life, this moment."

"Cappen, us 'll get out of the wai, quicksticks. It goo'th to our hearts, to zee 'un blading so. But, to vare up they stones again, is beyond our breeches."

"Fare out this way, then; across the water. But tell me first how the young man fell, and what his name is, and where he lives."

"'Twor all by rason of the bottled beer, sir. Do'e see thiccy moot-stoon, round the cornder? Us had a score of bottled beer, up yonner; and young Squire Dicky's hat were too small to hold 'un. Squire Dicky Touchwood, to Touchwood Park. Whatever will my lady zay to us?"

"You had better, go and see; but tell her not to be uneasy. The doctor will be here at once; and the lad will soon come round. Clear out, this very instant, dogs and men."

For by this time, thirty dogs, of every genealogy, were poking about, among the captain's pots.

CHAPTER VIII.

COLONEL WESTCOMBE.

WHILE the sportive Cantab thus broke into Mr. Arthur's humble greenhouse, his sister Julia was enjoying the keen air of the western moors, and passing through it swiftly, and sweetly, with the cheerful aid of a well-bred horse. Miss Touchwood always looked well in the saddle; and a lady's riding-habit was a graceful dress at that time, although the hat was hideous. But this young lady, thinking for herself, would not wear the hideous hat; but designed, in lieu thereof, a sensible and becoming head-gear, and got it made at Devonport. With its curving rim turned up at one side, and a grey feather pluming round the front, without any monstrous buckle, it sat lightly over her long dark eyebrows, clear eyes, and expressive face.

"What a booty her be!" said a tramp, to whom she had thrown a shilling, graciously.

"So her maight be," his wife replied, "so long as her getteth her own way."

Riding with her, across the moor, was her host, and godfather, Colonel Westcombe, a plain, stout man, of average stature, thick-set, broad across the back, and looking as if no tailor's art could make his clothes sit well to him. But that consideration moved him not, so long as he had plenty of room inside them. He thought of appearances, no more than " Captain Larks " himself did; though he liked to see ladies nicely dressed, and young men looking tidy. Upon his face, his character was as clearly outlined as his nose—a distinct, and eloquent feature. Any one could see, that he was simple-minded, slow at working out the twists of thought, accustomed to let his ideas flow into the mould of words, before dealing with them, gently reluctant to think evil of mankind, concerning any matter, in which he had not as yet been robbed atrociously, compassionate, fearless, and as hopeful as a child, and properly indignant when he came across a rogue. But large as the field was for that right feeling, (even in those more upright days), the Colonel was larger than to stay there very long; for his knowledge of the world must not harden him so much.

After many years of scrimped penurious life, such as behoves the British officer (especially when he has done great things, and must pay for the honour of doing them) this Colonel suddenly came into possession of large property. Diggory Westcombe, his father's elder brother, (who never would have anything to do with them in life, through some bitterness of blood), forgave upon his death-bed all the injuries he had done, and left all his property, when quite despaired of, to his next of kin, and right heir, Colonel John Westcombe.

That well-known warrior, and strong sharp-shooter against the sap-work of poverty, was amazed at being taken in the rear like this, and surrounded with an army bearing gifts. For a month of market-days, he was out of sorts, at not having to do his own marketing; for his clear sense told him, that what used to be economy, would now be no better than meanness. For the sake of his wife, whose health was weak, and of his son, who had the world before him, he was bound to rejoice at this access of wealth; but for himself, as he was laid upon the shelf, he would rather have rested on an oaken, than a golden one.

"If you please, Uncle John," said his fair

god-daughter, who had leave to call him so, though she was only of church-kin to him; "I cannot allow you to stay in this silent mood, which is growing over you."

"My dear, I beg your pardon," he answered, with his simple courtesy, and pleasantness; "I am sure, I would have talked, if I had anything to say. But surely with all this noble prospect —hills, and valleys, and watercourses, and the gorse coming out, and the sheep, and the ponies —you would much rather look about, than talk.

"Not for a moment; I am used to all that. It comes, and goes, just the same, and tells me nothing. I would rather have one of your stories of the war, than all the hills of Dartmoor, and the valleys full of water, and the sheep, that must terminate in tough mutton. And the beauty of your stories is that they must be true; because you always tell them, in the very same words, and with the very same look, every time."

"What a prosaic companion you have got! They say that Charles II. told his stories always so; but I hope that I resemble him, in few other points. Now, which of my stories do you wish me to begin?"

"The two, Uncle John; the famous pair,

which you promise to tell, when you have had
a good dinner. You must know the two I mean,
as well as I do. The first is, about the bravest
man you ever met with; and the second ought
to be, about the noblest man. The one I have
heard always makes me proud of being born in
England. I would rather hear such, than see
fifty miles of moorland, or even a waterfall fifty
feet high; because they stir me into great ideas,
without making me seem small. Oh, how can
poor Dicky spend the best of his time in rat-
hunting?"

"Different people look at things, from different
points of view, my dear," said the colonel, who
liked a rat-hunt himself, and also was fond of a
waterfall, and a fine view from the saddle. For
although he never noticed things, particularly
much, he was pleased that they should pass by
him nicely, without obliging him to think, any
more than change of air might do. "As long
as I can remember, Julia, I have been an
admirer of fine landscapes; and, indeed, I saw
very beautiful things, in Spain; yet I do not
know enough about such matters, to deny that—
that what you may call human affairs should
have the preference. Certainly the bravest man,
I ever yet have met with——"

"Uncle John, if you dare to begin it like that, you will flounder before you have come to the snuff place; and if you were to hesitate, you would begin to shake my perfect faith in it."

"Julia, is it possible that you can entertain the mere shadow of a doubt, about the very least particular? If I could imagine, that you did that, you should never again—I mean that I should never take any further pleasure, in relating to you that, or any other fact again."

"Now, Uncle John, you really must not be so exceedingly savage, and peppery. You begin to remind me of—well, never mind."

"My dear," said the colonel, "I beg your pardon heartily, if I have hastily expressed myself. I am well aware, that I sometimes do so; since I came into what people will insist upon calling my improved position. But I never mean anything by it, my dear child; and I am always sorry afterwards."

"Then you have no right to be so, and ought to go on more. Your only fault is, that you are too fond of letting people triumph over you. But now be quick, that's a dear Uncle John, and make amends by beginning it aright. You know that it always begins, like this,—' Towards the close of the hardest, perhaps, of the many hard conflicts our great commander'—but stop, till I come the right way of the wind."

"I am not at all sure," her companion answered, as the young lady drew her horse to the leeward side of his, and looked at him, with an encouraging smile; "that it is in my power to do justice to that remarkable little incident, while I am riding a fast-trotting horse. I was thoroughly used to a horse in my youth, for my father did afford to keep one, and I was on his back perpetually. And in the Peninsula, I have ridden some thousands of miles, with despatches. But, for five-and-twenty years, since I have not been wanted, our circumstances did not permit of much riding; and it takes a little time to be comfortable again."

" You ride like a Centaur, Uncle John. It is impossible for anybody to ride better. But still I can easily understand, that you like to do things in the regular way. Look, here are two great stones that seem to have dropped from the sky, on purpose to be sat upon. Suppose we jump off, and rest the horses; and you can enjoy all the landscape, while you talk."

By the side of the long and lonely track, these hoary granite blocks invited the traveller to a breezy rest. A tranquil mind would not have found that invitation marred, because accepted, through long ages now, by those who have the rest, without the breeze. The stones are the well-known " Coffin-stones; " whereat, for more than six hundred years, the bearers of the dead across the moor have halted from their heavy plod, laid down their burden on the stones, to take its latest stretch of mountain, and spread their own bodies on the grass around, to talk of what would happen to themselves ere long. Of these things the young lady had no knowledge, else would she never have sat down there; neither did her companion know; but the knowledge would not have moved him, more than to make him sit bare-headed.

" Let the poor things graze; the grass is sweet," he said, as he took the bridles off; and the nags, after jerking their noses with surprise, pricked their ears forward—not enough for him to catch them—and looked at him with well-meaning doubt. " Yes, you go, and crop, I say. The Lord has given you good teeth. And be sure you come at once, when you hear me whistle."

Obedient to his voice, they went, with a little tenderness of step at first, because it was long since they had crushed the blade; but presently the joy of nature's colour, and the taste, broke forth in them; they pranced, and threw up their heels, and capered; and the gentleman's horse made his stirrups clash beneath him, then fearing to waste one precious moment, they fell to, and worked the best mowing machine that has ever been invented. The colonel, more happy than a king, smiled at them, rested on his elbow, and began his tale.

" Towards the close of the hardest, perhaps, of the many hard conflicts our great commander won, by the aid of a gracious Providence, and his own unwearied vigilance; although the position of the enemy was turned, and the issue of the day scarcely doubtful, one very important post held out, and had repulsed all our attempts to carry it. The difficulties of the ground were great; not only was the approach very steep, and intersected by a watercourse, but also the French artillery, beautifully served, at grapeshot range, poured a crossing fire upon our attack. ' At the same time, our own guns could not be brought to bear, with any good effect, upon this crest, which was defended with admirable spirit, by a body of seasoned veterans, as calm, and steady, as our very best brigade.

In short, there seemed no chance of carrying the position, without fearful sacrifice; or even with it.

"The line of the enemy, as I have said, was being driven in, at almost every other point; and our great commander, perceiving that we must eventually obtain this post, sent orders that, as we could not take it, we should maintain our position, until the post was taken for us.

"Gentlemen,—or rather I should say, 'my dear,'—it is impossible for me to make you understand, what the feeling of our division was, when we received that message."

"Yes, Uncle John, I can understand it thoroughly. I should have been ready to knock my head, against the first French cannon I could find. But here you always take a pinch of snuff, with permission of the ladies, if any are present. You have my permission, and more than that, my orders. You will never take that post, without it."

"I know how incapable I am," resumed the colonel, in a loftier tone, "of describing the condition of· the human mind; but all around me being Englishmen—or, at least, an English lady—I need only say, that we were vexed. Because we had always supposed ourselves—

whether rightly, or wrongly, is not for me to say—to be the flower of the whole British army. Every man of us was burning to be at it, once again; and yet we knew better, than to set at nought our orders, by attempting another direct assault. I remember, as if I were looking at him now, how the indomitable General H——turned from the staff-officer, and spat upon the ground, to save himself from swearing at our great commander. But while we were all of us as red as a rocket, a young fellow, who had lately joined our division, a lieutenant in the 'Never mind what Hussars,' as we called them from their recklessness, came sheepishly up to our General H——, and asked for a private word with him. The general knew something of his family, I believe; and that makes no small difference, even with the strictest discipline. So, in spite of his temper, which was very bad just then, he led the young man apart; and presently came back, with his usual smile recovered, while the young man remounted his horse, and rode away.

"To us, it had been a most irksome thing, to wait there, doing nothing, but hearing in the distance the laughter of the enemy, and receiving, now and then, a round shot; and when there was a call for some forty volunteers, who could handle an axe, and haul trees away, the only trouble was to choose the men. Having been lucky enough to do something, which pleased the general, that morning, and being rather supple-jointed in those days, I obtained the command of this little detachment, under very simple orders. Our duty was nothing more than to draw three corks, as the general said, with a laugh at his own wit; and I never draw a cork now, or get it done for me—since I lost the right of doing my own work—without thinking, what a hard job it was, on that occasion.

" It seems, that the young man, I told you of just now, was very fond of wandering among the woods alone, whenever he could get the opportunity, without actual breach of orders; and he had just recognized the spur of the hill, which the enemy held so stubbornly, as a spot well known to him from a former visit. And unless his memory deceived him altogether, a narrow neck of land would be found, running down slantwise from the hill on our right, into the very heart of the position. With a hundred, or a hundred and fifty horse, dashing down upon the guns, while engaged in front, the whole must fall into our hands at once. Only there was no possibility of a charge, while three young cork-trees, which stood upon the neck, at its narrowest point, were standing.

"Now the difficulty was, as you will see at once, if you honour me by following my story, gentlemen, not only to cut down those three trees, but to get them clean out of the way, ere ever the enemy should have time to learn what was intended, and bring their guns to bear in that direction. In such a case, cavalry crowded together would simply be blown away, like wads; so that we were forced to go to work very warily, taking advantage of the sham attack in front.

"The trees were quite young, and the softness of the bark dulled the sound of our axes, as well as their edge; and being partly sheltered from the outlook of the enemy, by the form of the ground, we were getting on quite nicely, and had cleared away two of the trees, and felled the third, and were rolling it out of the way, before giving the signal for the charge, when the whistle of grape-shot told us that we had been discovered. One man fell, and we lifted him aside, that the horses might not tread on him; and then at any risk, I gave the

signal; because it must be now or never. Our
volunteers were ordered to slip off, right and
left, as two other guns were brought to bear on
us; but my duty compelled me, very much
against my liking, to stop in the middle of the
drift, to show our cavalry where the obstruction
was. For the smoke was hanging low upon
the ground, just like a fog.

"Now while I stood there, without any consideration, and spread out like a finger-post—
for I had not the courage to be careful—the
enemy sent another volley up the drift, and
much of it fell to my share. So that if they
had measured their powder aright, I had never
lived to find fault with it. Down I went, just
in the stream of the track, and for three months
heard no more of it.

"But the men at the side, who were out of
the way, gave a very clear history of what
happened, when the shower of grape went past
them. The charge, which must have trampled
me to death, was stopped by the young officer
commanding, with a wave of his sword, and his
horse reined across; and then he leaped off, and
came alone to where I lay. In the thickest of
the fire, he lifted me, they said, as calmly as a
nurse takes a baby from the cradle, and placed

me behind the cork-tree, where shot could never touch me, and the hoof must turn aside. Then he tore off the scarf from his neck, and bound up a wound, that was draining my body: while the Frenchmen perceived him, as the smoke rolled off, and like truly noble fellows, forbore their fire. He kissed his hand to them, in acknowledgment of this; and then shouting to them that the fighting was resumed, returned to his horse, gave the signal to charge, and carried their guns in a twinkling. Now, such a deed as that makes one proud to be an Englishman."

"Or even a good Frenchman," fair Julia replied. "I scarcely know, which of them behaved the best. And though you make so little of your own part, I think you were the hero of the whole thing, Uncle John. But of course you found out the young officer's name? And now for the other story, Uncle John. I have heard this story of the bravest man, a lot of times; and I like it better almost every time. But I have never heard the story of the noblest man; and I dare say that is finer still."

"It is," the colonel answered, in his simple way. "But I never like to tell that tale, in cold blood, or before my dinner. And even so, I must have people, who can enter into it. And even then, one ought to have a heavy cold, to explain the condition of the eyes that comes of it."

" The heavy cold you will certainly have; if you sit on these cold stones so long. And here comes a hailstorm, the delicate attention of soft April to Dartmoor. Oh, I shall be blind, if it goes on like this. Whistle for the horses, uncle, dear."

CHAPTER IX.

THE RED-FACED MAN.

BEFORE " the ever loyal city," as Exeter loves to call itself, was undermined with iron bars, beneath its castle-ramparts, Northernhay was a quiet place, aside of the noisy London road, and pleasant for a Sunday walk. Here, in a good old ivied house, snugly encompassed by thick cob walls, was living, and well deserved to live, a gentleman of the ancient name of " Tucker." Also his Christian name was ancient; being " Caleb," and no more.

This gentleman lived with his widowed sister, Mrs. Giblets, late of Barnstaple, whose two boys went to the high grammar-school, as often as they could not help it. The deceased Mr. Giblets, a currier of repute, had thrice been Mayor of Barnstaple, and had sacrificed his life to his festive duties, at the time of the Reform Bill. His relict was a lady of like dignity, and

virtue, convinced (as all Barum people are) of
the vast superiority of that town; yet affable
to the Mayor of Exeter. Their daughter, Mary
Giblets, was a very nice young lady, a thorough
girl of Devon, with a round rosy face, a smile
for everybody, and almost at everything, a pair
of brisk substantial feet, and a special turn for
marketing.

Caleb Tucker, the owner of the house, but
not the master always, had long been in business, as a timber-merchant, and still would make
a purchase, or a sale, upon occasion, although
he had retired from the firm, which he had
reared. Honesty, industry, enterprise, and
prudence, had won for him nearly quite enough
of money, to live upon happily, and want no
more. In the vigour of life, when the hearts
of men are as quick of warmth, as a fire at its
prime, he had incurred a very serious loss,
never to be balanced in £ s. d. The wife of
his love, and the little ones of theirs, went all
to the grave, between a Sunday and a Saturday,
through a storm of fever, called in Devonshire
" the plague." This sorrow took the zeal out
of his existence, and left him a grave, well-
balanced man, who had learned that the poise of
life is not troy-weight.

Now, in the holiday of calm age, Caleb Tucker
was a venerable person; slow to move, except
with pity; and tranquil in the steadfast hope
of finding, in a larger world, the losses of this
little one.   His sister was twenty years younger
than himself, and her children were his succes-
sors; and he meant to do his duty to his own
kin, instead of founding charities, to be jobbed
by aliens.   Under these circumstances, it was
right of Mrs. Giblets, to make much of him, and
encourage him to save, and increase, his cash.

"How sudden the changes of the weather
seem to be!" he was saying to his sister, as
they sat out in the garden, on the Saturday,
the very day after the colonel's tale had been
hurried by the hailstorm; "the spring weather
never used to change like this; at least when
the turn of the days was over.   How bright it
was yesterday, until it began to rain!   Then
the hills, towards Dartmoor, were covered with
snow, or hail, or whatever it may have been."

"It must have been either hail, or snow, if
it was white," Mrs. Giblets replied, being proud
of perfect accuracy; "the weather is continually
changing; but the only white things in it are
snow, and hail."

"Certainly, Mollikins, and frost as well.   It

might have been the white frost on the moors. But whatever it was, it made me think, this morning, as I looked at it from my bedroom window, of that poor gentleman I bought the land for. He has made such a beautiful garden up there, and I fear that the frost will destroy all his bloom."

"He must suffer the will of the Lord, I suppose; as everybody else is obliged to do. Sometimes I lose my patience with him; because you never tell me, who he is. Why should a gentleman come down here, and buy a little far-off place like that, and work like a common labourer? No one would dare to attempt such a thing, in the neighbourhood of Barnstaple. It would be the duty of the mayor, to find him out. But in this part of the world, conspirators carry on, just as they please."

"Sister, you talk a great deal too fast. If you ever know the truth, you will be sorry for your words. Women are so fond of rushing to the worst conclusions."

"Some of them do so; but whose fault is it? You know that I do the very opposite, Caleb, whenever I am not denied the knowledge. I wish, with all my heart, that I had never heard about him; although I liked him very much, the only time I saw him. But I always take things, as I find them. I have no curiosity whatever, about anything."

"Molly, you are very wise," answered Mr. Tucker; "we have all of us enough of trouble, with our own affairs. And here comes pretty Mary, for to tell us something pleasant."

"No, indeed, uncle, it is quite the other way," cried Mary, as she hurried up the walk, from the side-door; "I took the short cut, and I left all the nuts I was buying for Bob, and for Harry, to tell you not to see the man—or the gentleman at least, who is riding up the hill, to look for you. Oh, uncle, dear, he is such a nasty man; and has the evil eye, if ever anybody had it! Oh dear, I turned my Testament in my pocket—mischief will come of it, as sure as I'm alive."

"If ever there was a little goose, in the King's, or rather, in the Queen's dominions now, her name is Mary Giblets." Though he spoke thus bravely, Mr. Tucker did not like it; and his sister said—

"Mary, fie for shame! Look at your gathers, Miss!"

"I had no time to think about anything at all," she answered, with her colour ripened, from the peach-bloom into peach; " he was asking at Besley's, and Snell's, and Sharland's, where Mr. Caleb Tucker lived; and he called you ' the land-agent.' Mr. Snell told him, you had never been that, but a strictly retired gentleman; and then the man laughed—such a nasty laugh, mamma; and young Tom Besley, who is always such a stupid, looked up from the copper mill, where he was grinding pepper, and he says, ' That young lady will show you, sir; that's his own niece, Miss Giblets.' I felt, as if I could have boxed his ears. And the red-faced man rode up to me, with his hat off, and said, ' Miss Giblets, will you be my charming guide?' And I couldn't think of anything to say; he looked so impudent. But I made him a curtsy, and began walking up the hill; and then I thought to myself, that I would pay him out. So I turned down Black Horse Alley, towards the cut across parson's meadow (which is the nearest way, you know) and left him to follow, or not, as he pleased. Well, it pleased him to come, and to want to talk to me; just as if I were nothing but a shop-girl. I looked at him, over my shoulder, now and then; and said yes and no, for a quarter of a mile; and likely, he considered me as stupid as Tom Besley. Then suddenly, we came upon the high turn-stile of parson's meadow, where the bull is; and I slipped through, like anything. 'Halloa! Do you expect me to ride over this?' he said. And I said, 'Oh dear! Oh dear! How very stupid of me! But you only asked me for the shortest way, sir. I dare not stop, to give you any more directions, because of the bull, in the bottom of the ham.' And away I ran, and here I am."

"My darling, what a risk to run! I have told you not to do it," her mother exclaimed, as she finished her tale; "that bull has tossed three people."

"I am ten times more afraid of a bad man, than a bull. Now be sure that you refuse to see him, Uncle Caleb."

"My dear," said Mr. Tucker, "you are scarcely old enough, to be reproached with want of reason. I dare say, the gentleman has no harm in him; although he may be a little forward. If so, he had his match in a very modest girl; though one of strong prejudices, I am afraid. Let us go into the house; perhaps he will be here directly."

Before they had time to put their garden-chairs away, the rusty wire beneath the thatch of the warm cob-wall, that sheltered them, gave a slow, reluctant, creaking jerk, and then a quick rattle, as it was pulled again ; and the big bell, swinging in the ivy of the house-porch, threw up its mouth, like a cow about to bellow, and fell back upon its wagging tongue, through a rustle of crisp leafage. " Let him ring again," said Mr. Tucker ; " when a man is in a hurry, I have known it do him good. Don't go away, sister ; I will see him here. I am too old a soldier, to be carried by storm, in this way. Mary, you be off, my dear ; as if the bull was after you."

Miss Giblets withdrew, but much against her will, for she had a fine stock of healthy curiosity, and had made up her mind, that the red-faced man was come upon an interesting errand. Then Bill, the boy of all work, came grinning, with a card in one hand, and a shilling in the other. " A' gied me this," he said, showing first the shilling, as the more important object of the two. " Be I to kape 'un, or gie 'un to you ? "

" Gie 'un to your mother," replied his master, as he took the card, and read the words " Mr. George Gaston," with no address beneath them.

" Ha, sir, and how are you to-day ? " The

visitor shouted, with a hearty voice. "I have taken the liberty of following my pasteboard. I hope I see the lady quite well also. Madam, your servant! I am quite old-fashioned. I glory in the society of the ladies; but my manners are comparatively out of date, I fear."

The widow of the mayor possessed a shrewd tongue, as well as a stately reserve, sometimes; and the former was burning to say, that the sooner such manners were positively out of date, the better. Like her daughter, the lady conceived an extraordinary hatred of this man, at sight; but she only showed it, by a careful bow, and a gaze of reasonable surprise.

"Excuse me, sir—Mr. Gaston, I suppose," said Caleb Tucker, rising slowly, and lifting his hat from his silvery curls; "but I doubt not that, if you are come upon business, you have brought me a letter of introduction; I do very little in the way of business now, and only with people, who are known to me. And I have not the honour of remembering your name."

"You are quite right. Everything you do is right, according to the account I have received of you. Shall I take this chair? But it would make me wretched, to think that I had banished Mrs. Tucker."

"That lady is my sister, sir—Mrs. Giblets, formerly of Barnstaple."

"Bless my heart! I never heard of such a thing. Have I met Mrs. Giblets at last, without knowing her? My cousin, Sir Courtenay, is always speaking of her, and her graceful, and refined hospitality. But too exclusive—he told me as much. Like all the superior ladies, you are too exclusive, Mrs. Giblets."

"That charge has been brought against me, I confess," the lady replied with dignity; "but wherever would you be, sir, without you drew a line, between wholesale, and retail?"

Mrs. Giblets retired, with a gracious bow, but some doubt still about the good faith of the visitor; for although he was older than herself, as her conscience (which she always consulted on the subject) told her, he wore a red-striped neckerchief, and a cut-away coat, of bright green, with gilt buttons. Moreover, his voice was loud and harsh, his manner too bold, his figure burly, and his gestures impatient, and almost imperious; while his face, though resolute and rather handsome, expressed, more than impressed, good opinion of himself. His forehead was high and square, his eyes piercing but not steadfast, his nose strong and aquiline, and chin very

firm, and prominent. But the colour of the
cheeks was fiercely red, the mouth very wide
and voracious; and instead of a curve at the
hinges of the jaws, there occurred a conspicuous
angle. Boys, who have powers of observation,
happily extinguished in later life, dubbed him
at school, "George Coffin-face;" but when his
brow expanded, the name no longer suited him,
except as regards the part below the ears, where
a few white whiskers showed the harshness of
the angle, now become more prominent, from
years of zealous exercise; while his very florid
colour, and thick crop of tawny hair, gave
abundance of life to his countenance.

"No, Mr. Tucker, I have ridden a long way,"
he began, after looking round, and bringing his
chair nearer, "upon a matter, really of no importance to me, in any other light than this—
that I may do a kindness, and help a fellow-
creature. Probably, I shall not even earn so
much as thanks; and you know how little those
are worth. I do not pretend to be moved by
any Quixotic ardour, or Christian duty, or
broad philanthropy, or any romantic motive.
But a sense of gratitude for a good turn done
me, five-and-twenty years ago, together with
some natural desire to baffle selfish roguery—

although it is no concern of mine, you see— has led me to sacrifice some valuable time, and trespass perhaps on yours, sir."

"Not at all. Don't speak of it. I am glad to be of service," Mr. Tucker replied, in his regular way. "But did I understand, that you had brought a letter to me?"

"Not a syllable of any kind. I make a point of never insulting anybody. And to suppose that a man, of your experience, could fail to know a gentleman at first sight, would be most impertinent. And let me remind you," continued Mr. Gaston, perceiving that the other looked a little glum at this, "that I am not come, upon any business question, where my solvency, and so on, might require to be established. My object is simply to perform a kindness; and your aid will cost you nothing, neither risk a single penny. I ask you no favour; I simply propose it, as a duty to yourself, that you should enable me to confer a benefit, upon a most deserving, and ill-treated fellow-Christian. Instead of losing anything by it, you will gain very largely. For you will thus restore to position, and some wealth, a man of most grateful, and generous nature. I have no cant about me, and it is my abhorrence; but it would be too much of the opposite extreme, to deny that the hand of a good Providence is here."

"Sir, you speak well, and very sensibly so far;" answered the cautious timber-merchant, trying to conquer his unreasonable dislike of the red-faced gentleman at first sight; "if you will kindly tell me, what it is that I can do, I will do it, unless there should be reason to the contrary, or at any rate necessity for consideration."

"Oh, it does not require half a moment's hesitation; you will say that I have made much ado about nothing. All I want to know, is the address of a gentleman, for whom you bought a small estate, from fifteen to twenty years ago; probably the shorter date is the more correct one—rather a tall man, with a military manner."

"I am not a land-agent," Mr. Tucker replied; " neither do I meddle with the lawyer's business. But at one time, from my knowledge of the county, and purchase of timber, and so on, I was frequently asked to obtain a purchaser for small outlying properties, perhaps belonging to the gentlemen, who were selling me their timber. Of course, the matter afterwards passed through the proper hands; and I never thought of making any charge for what I did. Still

there were so many cases, that without par-
ticulars, I cannot pretend to say anything."

"But, you must have known, in almost every
case, who the purchaser was, what made him
buy, where he lived, what he did with himself,
&c. Officers seldom turn farmers, I believe,
and seldom have managed, from their miserable
pay, to save money to buy land with."

"I am ready to oblige you, Mr. Gaston, if I
can, without any breach of confidence. Your
inquiry is unusual, as you must know; and
unless you can manage to be more precise, I see
no possibility of helping you. If you can supply
me with the name, and date, I may have some
recollection of the matter you refer to. Also it
is only fair to ask, how you have heard of me,
and my share in the business. You can scarcely
consider that question rude."

"Certainly not, my dear sir," replied the
visitor; "everything is plain, and above board
here. I only regret, that from my own ignorance,
I should have to give you so much trouble.
But in your desire to do good, you will excuse
me. The case has some little peculiarities;
which, with your permission, I will recount.
Only, let me ask you first, if you are sure that a
long tale will not weary you."

"Nothing will weary me about—I mean in a case of so much interest."

"How good of you, to feel such interest without any knowledge of the people implicated! But alas, Mr. Tucker, I am suffering from thirst. I have ridden nearly fifty miles, since noon; now all very pure air, such as that of Devon, contains saline particles; and in the distance, I behold a pump. I would crave your hospitable leave, to go, and move the handle."

"Mr. Gaston, I humbly beg your pardon," said the ancient gentleman, arising with a sigh; "but my mind is not as present to me, as it used to be. We have not the name of inhospitality, as a rule, in Devonshire; but I give you my honour, sir, that it quite escaped me. And after your ride—what will my sister say? I beg you to come into our little parlour. It is getting rather cold out here, and not so comfortable. Perhaps you have never even dined? Oh dear!"

"I shall go to the pump, and that alone, if you say another syllable, my dear sir. But if you make a point of it, I will go in. But, nothing to eat, sir—not one morsel. My dinner is a trifle to a man like me; and I have made arrangements about it. Anything, anything—

a glass of cold water, with a quarter of a knob · of sugar, suits me well."

However, like most men who speak thus, the traveller was better in his deed, than word; so that three large tumblers of hot rum and water confessed him more capacious than themselves, before he had much to say to them.

"It is a curious story. You misdoubted me out there," he began, with a wave of his glass drumstick towards the garden. "But, Tucker, I have found you now, to be a hearty fellow. The heart, after all, is the real driving power with good fellows, such as you and I are. Hang it, I don't suppose, one man in fifty thousand would have taken up this thing, like me, from pure love of the specie."

"Of the human species," his host amended gently; then, fearful of any rudeness, added— "no doubt you are right, however; the two words are much the same, I do believe."

"To me no matter is of any moment," resumed the red-faced man, with his roses deepening into mulberries, "in comparison with the glow of heart, produced by a noble action. And when we can benefit ourselves as well, what a poor heart it must be, that hesitates! Look at the case, which I have in hand. An amiable but eccentric man, a pattern of every virtue, except the rare one of common sense, takes a turn against all his family! He fancies that they are all set against him, that their views are sordid, and his alone are large; that, as he cannot alter them, his best plan is, to have nothing to do with them, and keep out of their sight. Also he believes, that a man's truest work is, to earn his own living, with his own hands, and wash them clean of all the vices of the world. In a word, he has crotchets, about society, nature, and things of that sort, to put it clearly. Well, he disappears, without rhyme or reason, having lost the only link that retained him in society, a charming young wife, who was a beauty of this county. He buries himself, in some outlandish region, although he belongs to a distinguished family, and has done a good deal to distinguish himself. No doubt, he believes that he has acted for the best; that he is fulfilling what is called in the cant of the day, " a lofty mission ; " that he stood across the light of other people's prospects, and was bound in duty to obliterate himself; whereas, in reality, he is consulting his own tastes, which are out of all reason, and fantastic.

" Let us say, that his family have long looked

upon him as an excellent, but misguided fellow; not a black sheep, but a stray sheep, which will have its own way; and hoping for his happiness, they make no fuss about him. But in the course of years, he becomes more needful; as a snug little property falls to him by succession, and his signature is needed, as a matter of formality, in a settlement of importance. In such a case, he must abandon for a moment his hermitage, receive his dues, and perform his duty. Possibly, he may be induced to return altogether to civilized existence. If so, he will be welcomed by enthusiastic friends, and his history shall appear, in letters of pure gold. On the other hand, if he prefers the seclusion, which must have become his second nature now, he may return to it, with his wheels greased—excuse the coarseness of the allusion, my dear sir; what I mean is, with more butter for his farmhouse bread. Now, what do you think of my proposal?"

"I do not appear to have quite understood," Mr. Tucker replied, very quietly, and slowly, "what proposal there is before me; or even that there is any at all. If not a rude question, in my own house, I would venture to ask, sir, without offence, whether you are a solicitor?"

"Come now, my friend, you are a little too

hard on me. When I have tried to make it clear to you, that I desire to do good!"

"I am sure I beg your pardon, sir. But so they may sometimes; I do assure you, I have known it. But since you are not in the law, I may speak freely. And to save you further trouble, I will own right out, that I am pretty sure, by this time, of the gentleman you mean. I know of no great mystery in the matter; and such things are not at all in my line. He wished to be quiet, and undisturbed, as a man might well do in a sad affliction; and as every man has a right to do, if he chooses. I felt the same feeling myself, Mr. Gaston, in the days when the Lord afflicted me."

The voice of the old man trembled slightly, for his affliction was life-long; and this had helped to draw him towards the man in like distress, who had made up his mind, to retire from the world.

"You too have lamented?" said the red-faced man. "It is the lot of us all, my dear sir. But the duty of the strong man is, to up, cast off, and gird himself."

"I will not deny it. But it takes a time to do it, as well as a clear view of the world. And for looking at the world, there are quite as many hills, as there are men to stand on them. But I am keeping you long from your dinner, Mr. Gaston, which I believe you have ordered. You do not expect me to tell you, I suppose, all I know about the gentleman you ask of?"

"If there is anything that I avoid, Tucker," the visitor replied, as he compounded for himself a fourth instalment of rum-punch—"it is the barest semblance of a liberty. Your excellent health, my dear friend! I have never encountered a more harmonious soul. No, no; I only ask you, for the gentleman's address, to do him a genuine, and great kindness."

"It will give me real pleasure," said the host, who was standing, and bowing at the generous carousal in his honour, " to place you in communication with him; upon the receipt of his permission. That is a thing for him to give; and not for me to take as granted. Shall I write, and inform him of your application? Or will you write yourself, Mr. Gaston, and leave it with me to be forwarded? You do not know the name, I think you say—the present name of the gentleman. But if you will use the name you know him by, I will answer for safe delivery. We may save the post, if you begin at once. Here is all you want, including sealing-wax;

and I will leave the room while you write, if
you think proper."

" Well!" cried the visitor, jumping up, with a
force that shook the room, and made the glasses
rattle, while his face turned white, and its glow
flew to his eyes; "is that all you mean to tell
me?"

" I can tell you nothing more," the old man
answered, looking at him firmly, but with great
surprise; " nothing more; until I get permission. Surely you would not——"

" I forgot one little thing," the other interrupted, as he thrust his hand so violently into
a breast-pocket, that the host nearly made up his
mind to see a pistol; " I forgot that nothing is
to be had for nothing. My mind is so set upon
discovering that man, that if fifty pounds—well
then, a hundred pounds——"

" Not a thousand, sir ; no, nor fifty thousand,"
Caleb Tucker broke in sternly. " You must be
a heartless man, whatever you may say about
your heart, to insult me so. It is lucky for you,
that I am not a young man. Leave my house.
I am not accustomed to entertain such visitors."

" Over-righteous Caleb," said the red-faced
man, recovering his colour, and his temper, or
enough of it to supply cool insolence; " we have

no faith in all this noble indignation. You know, my remarkably stingy host, upon which side your bread is buttered. And you think to make a good thing, of what you have got out of me. Ta, ta, Master Dry-rot! Your very cheap rum has spoiled my appetite for dinner. I shall go to your cathedral, and pray to be delivered from the company of ancient hypocrites."

CHAPTER X.

ANGELIC PEEPS.

In the waxing of the moon, there are great things done, upon this world of moonshine. Then is the time, to plant the vine, the medlar, and the apple-tree, to ring the store-pig, to inaugurate the capon, and rope the roguish onion—crafty contraband of maiden's lips. Then also, is the time for loftier, and more subtle enterprise; to tempt, or steal, the shy young glance—the flutter of inquiring eyes, the touch clandestine, the irrelevant remark, the sigh about nothing, yet productive of a blush, the blush that increases the confusion it betrays— and a million other little ways of wonder, in the wondrous maze of love.

Even so, and with a multitude of pieces of 16 oz. glass—so called in the trade, but really never more than 14 oz.—sticking in his wounds, with the putty still upon it, Dicky Touchwood

came to himself; and lost it, ere ever he had
time to scratch it; which is the first of all
bodily instincts. For over him leant the very
loveliest creature, ever seen out of a dream, or
in it. Deep compassion, sweet anxiety, and an
inborn dread of the coroner, or the doctor who
precedes him, filled the beautiful eyes of Rose
Arthur. The youth looked up, and had a very
clear idea of having flown up, to what our poets
call " the blue."

" Hush!" the maiden whispered, as his lips
began to move; "keep your head upon the
flower-pot, and try to think of nothing. Never
mind, about all the things you have broken.
You did not mean to do it, and it can't be
helped now. The only thing you have to do, is
to keep as still as possible. Papa is gone to
meet Dr. Perperaps, and he may be expected, at
any moment. You are to go to sleep, until he
comes."

The heavily wounded youth, instead of obey-
ing orders, gazed the more. To look at her
was poetry, and to listen to her was music.
But she turned away, and left him nothing for
his eyes.

" It must have been an angel. But they
have no papas," he began to reason with him-

self aloud; "and they never would have sent for Dr. Perperaps. None but the devil could have sent for him. Oh, where can I be? What is the meaning of it? And what is this mysterious substance, all around me?"

"Brewer's grains," the silvery voice replied; "we have it every spring, to catch the slugs with; and my father put it down, to keep you cool, and moist. It smells very nice; you should be thankful for it."

"So I am. Oh, I am thankful now to be able to smell any beer at all. But I seem to be full of holes, and sore places, and pieces of stuff sticking into me!"

"You could hardly expect, to have no holes yourself, after making such a great hole in our glass; but you must not let that dwell at all upon your mind. My father is a gentleman, who does his own glazing. And really, if you must fall, you have fallen very luckily. Although, when first you look at it, it seems almost an enormous hole, for a smallish boy to have made so quickly."

Richard Touchwood, Esquire, jumped up, when he heard himself called "a smallish boy." Or rather, he tried to jump up, but his swathings stopped him, and then a very jagged barb of pain ; and then a light hand replanted him, among the grains, and upon the pot.

"You are too bad," she said; "you want to go everywhere, where you have no business. But oh, I am so sorry for your pain, poor boy! If you would only cry a little, it would do you so much good."

"Cry!" exclaimed Dicky, in a high tone of disdain, yet not wholly out of concert with the course suggested; "have you never even heard that I am a Caius-College man, the place where the very best physicians come from?"

"No, I never heard of that. I have heard of hospitals, and the wards that belong to them; but never of keys colleges. Since you are in training for the medical profession, you ought to try more than you do, to enter into your own position. It is a strict necessity, for you to lie still; but instead of doing that—— Oh, here comes Dr. Perperaps, crossing our bridge very nicely indeed! And he has brought his daughter, Spotty, with him. He never goes anywhere, without Miss Spotty. Now you will be in better hands than mine. Good-bye."

"Oh, I implore you not to go away. Whoever you are—and I have hardly seen you yet, although I have told you all about myself—do try to see that Dr. Perperaps doesn't kill me."

"Oh no! He is the most kind-hearted man; and exceedingly clever, for a doctor. And when he does happen to make a mistake, his daughter puts it right for him. They are very nice people, and so natural."

"Don't I know him too well? He pulled out my wrong tooth; and how could his daughter put it in again? I had a bad knee, and he blistered the other, to produce counter-irritation. And once, when a piece of camp-stool ran into me—— Oh, I had better hold my tongue! I know his footstep. I'll be dead—to save him trouble."

"Ah, ha! What have we here? Very sad indeed. Most serious case. Our valued young friend—let us turn him over. A spirited youth —too spirited, in fact. Our great universities produce a kind of comatosis. They over-tax corporeal, and relax the mental energies. The result of such a system is before us now."

Dr. Perperaps, as he came to this conclusion, turned to his daughter, who was standing in the doorway; and she said, "Yes. But he has tumbled through the glass."

"That is a minor, but a logical result, of the vicious system I describe. The physical powers have been overdone. The judgment was dormant; or he would not have tried the leap. Now both pay the penalty of disproportion. He does not know me, the truest friend he ever had. It is a beautiful instance of our interdependence."

"Here are the bandages," his daughter said concisely; "and here is cold water. We may be glad, Miss Arthur, of a little warm, if convenient."

"These hasty ways," the doctor whispered to Mr. Arthur, while his daughter set to work, "are entirely the result of the Reform Bill. Spotty was a good girl, until that passed; and so far as that goes, she is a good girl still. But it caused a feminine upheaval, sir; and the wisest man dare not predict the issue. She does the preliminaries; she is wonderfully sagacious; and then the scientific element steps in. Be careful, my dear; be very careful. Lady Touchwood thinks so much of him."

Spotty, who acted as her father's assistant, and better half in his profession, proceeded very strongly, and most skilfully, with her work; while the doctor serenely discussed the case.

The hapless rat-hunter had fainted in earnest,
at the very first symptom of medical relief; and
this was the best thing he could have done.
" His wounds were very interesting, and likely
to be painful ; but properly speaking, not really
dangerous to a Cambridge man. No limbs were
broken ; although the descent was calculated to
produce much fracture. And unless inflam-
matory action supervened, recovery was only a
question of time, and of skilful, and unremitting
curative appliances." Thus said the doctor;
and such was his report, by a boy upon a pony,
to Touchwood Park.

While these things were toward, and theory
and practice were kissing one another—as they
generally do, when the money goes into the
same bag—Rose was seeking, at her father's
order, a redoubtable person to lend a hand.
Captain Larks, with the instinct of a soldier,
knew that the medical proceedings would terminate in carrying, as they generally do.
Therefore, he got his hand-barrow ready, and
sent for an able-bodied man, to share the weight
of it. And this was a good workman, when he
liked to work, Sam Slowbury, of Brent-fuzz
corner.

Slowbury disliked all activity, as heartily as

anybody in the parish; and could shirk it, as thoroughly as any man. He entered well into the humour of the contract, in virtue of which a man gets as much money, on a Saturday night, for doing nothing, as for working hard throughout the week, and husbands at once his own resources, and prospective value, by prolonging his job to the uttermost penny.

Such was the integrity of this man, and his principles so uncompromising; so thoroughly did he respect himself, and dignify his vocation, that whether he were out of sight, or whether he were strictly watched, his behaviour was the same. In neither case, would he do a stroke of work, except as the exception. This conduct ensured him universal regard, and more work, than even he could leave undone.

After large, and sweet experience of the British workman, Mr. Arthur had come to the definite conclusion, that these are the men whom it is wisest to employ. Because there is no disappointment with them; no qualm of conscience, at neglecting to look after them; no loss of time, in absurd endeavours to make them do a little work, now and then. There are few greater pleasures, than to contemplate repose; especially when honourably purchased by oneself; and any employer of Sam Slowbury might always enjoy that pleasure in perfection. But Sam, to-day, was comparatively at work, having made up his mind to a holiday, and to spend it in the perilous pursuit of the rat. The catastrophe of that great expedition left his mind in a gentle, head-scratching condition, candidly open to a pint of cider; and here he stood now, at one end of the bier.

"Steady!" said the captain, a needless exhortation to a man of Sam's philosophy; then liting his end of the barrow, upon which the casual visitor had been laid, he led them, down the bloom-roofed alleys, to his cheerful cottage-door. For the green-house, under the cliff, was nearly two hundred yards from his dwelling-place.

"Pardon me, sir, if I speak amiss," said Dr. Perperaps, when they stopped here; "but may I ask you a somewhat important question, round the corner? Spotty, attend to the patient. Now, sir, it is this," he continued in a low tone, as soon as Mr. Arthur followed him, "we have reason to believe, that you value very highly, as every good Englishman has a right to do, your privacy, your retirement—I might say, your charming seclusion from the world. Now, this boy's mother, Lady Touchwood, is—ah well—you understand me."

"I have merely heard her name; I know nothing more about her. What is she, for me to be afraid of?"

"Not at all, my dear sir; you misunderstand me. Her ladyship is a delightful person, until —until her feelings overpower her. Charitable, kind-hearted, hospitable, devout, elegant in her manners, and fond of making presents—a very fine quality growing rarer every year,—still, she does want to get to the bottom of everything; doubtless from intensity of sympathy. And if anybody baffles her, she becomes the very devil. Pardon me, Captain Larks, I speak in strictest confidence; but I have reason to believe, that her ladyship's attention has been directed, with some interest, to you. If once she gets admission to your little household (which you cannot well deny her, if you take in her son), as soon as her alarm about him is over, she will begin to feel an undesirable interest, in everything concerning you."

"Dr. Perperaps," answered Mr. Arthur, "it is most obliging of you, to show such consideration for my wishes."

The doctor, a short, well rounded man, came

one step nearer, and behind the silver head of the black bamboo, which he always carried, relaxed his dignity with a wink.

"It is not altogether that," he said; "I consider my own convenience also. I am not so young as I was; and I don't want to walk up your hill, twice a day. And distance is a professional element. Touchwood Park is three times as far off; and a carriage would be sent for me. The patient may very well be taken, as he is, to my little residence, and go home, upon springs, in a day or two. His affectionate mother would send for me, twice every day; and with prophylactic, as well as remedial measures—— "

"I am much obliged to you; but it will not do. The boy has been wounded on my premises; and with me he shall stay, until his relatives remove him. I should feel that I had done an inhuman thing, if I sent him from my door, in his present condition. Say no more about it, sir; but come in, and help us."

The doctor gave in, as he could not help doing, but said to himself, that he should have his revenge; for he knew a little more of Lady Touchwood, than Captain Larks could dream of. And he saw a good chance of some pleasant excitement, and matters of deep interest to be told to his good wife, when Spotty, and the little ones, were gone to bed, and the toddy was being measured in the Apostle's spoon. Like nearly all medical men in country places, he had a hard time of it; being at everybody's beck, and call; and called for almost everything, except to take his money.

And so, when evening came down upon the hills, and the hills tried to pass it off in shadow to the valleys, there was no more comfortable fellow to be found, within the enclosure of their deepening folds, than little Dicky Touchwood at Larks' cot. By the strong arms of Spotty, and the nimble hands of Rose, a bed was provided for him, in the captain's sitting-room— a pretty little place, with a door opening into the span-roof vinery. Here lay the youth, upon the best bed of the cottage; with three bottles of mixture, tied over at the top with white, like sisters of mercy, and a basin of soup keeping warm, upon one of Mr. Arthur's devices for slaying green-fly; and best of all cordials—in his present state of heart—bright glimpses of the lovely Rose, that flitted to and fro.

He would have known better, than to let his

mind wander, about pretty figures, and after sweet faces, and into, and out, of a thousand vagaries of smile, and of sigh, and of tremulous delight, if the glass of the green-house had begun to hurt him yet, or the putty to torment him, as they meant to do to-morrow. For the present, he was grateful for every single hole made in him (so long as lard, and liniment, prevented it from smarting) as a trifle of punctuation, needful before the great impression of his life was struck.

"Now, Master Touchwood, how often must I tell you," said Spotty, who was left, to help as nurse, "that you are not to roll, like that? It loosens all the fastenings, and it will set up inflammation.

"I don't care two skips of a—flower, if it does. I must see my angel; and I can't see through the bed-post."

"I tell you once more, there is no angel here. The old women call me a ministering angel, when the parish allows them a noggin of gin. But I know well enough, that I am not angelic."

"As if I meant you!" the patient answered, with more sincerity than courtesy. "You are very kind indeed, and you rub up the rags, like silver paper, and you make them soft. But the other—oh, Miss Perperaps, what a perfect, perfect angel!"

"It is time for you to have this draught. Your tongue is white. That comes of talking about angels so. To make a face is useless. You must have it. I dare say it is nasty. Shall the angel come, and give it you?"

"Oh no! Please not to let her see me take it. I always make such horrid faces. And I want her to think, how nice I am. If I could only get it down, while she is round the corner."

"Wait, till I shake the bottom up. The best of the flavour is always there. Now take it, like a man; and I will let her know, how brave you were."

"But Spotty—or at least I mean, Miss Perperaps, do you think it will really make any difference with her? Are you sure that she will have a high opinion of me—if—if I do it?"

"I am certain that she will. She sighed, and she said 'Poor fellow!' twice over, when she saw the bottles come. If you wish to be a hero, put your head the proper way, and open your mouth, and shut both eyes."

So absorbing was the power of love at first

sight, that Dicky took his medicine like a martyr, and even pretended that he found it nice.

"Here is your reward! I will tell her of your goodness; how pleased she will be!" exclaimed his nurse; "because she knows so well, what a job it is to make you. She will hardly believe her own ears."

"I don't understand you. How can she know about it, when she never set eyes on me, before to-day?"

"I don't mean the angel," answered Spotty, with a laugh; "or at least, I mean your proper one—your dear mamma. Here comes Lady Touchwood."

"Oh, bother!" cried the young squire; "don't let her in. Say, that you've got orders—say, that it will kill me—say anything you like— say they're laying me out."

"Oh, Master Dicky, you ungrateful wretch! If I only had a mother, to make a fuss about me! Would I ever shut her out, that I might carry on with angels?"

Poor Spotty was the daughter of a departed Mrs. Perperaps; and her stepmother (having many interesting babes, of far greater value than Sporetta) employed that young lady, for

the best part of her time, in the genial occupa-
tions of the nursery, and wash-house. This
damsel, being gifted with a great love of the
healing art, was now beginning to revolt at
large, from the drudgery of pail, and pan; and
her father, who was not a fool (although he
used the jargon of that race), perceived, in this
daughter, a revival of the fine enthusiasm, which
had pulled him down. In the fervour of youth,
he had nourished gay ideas of making great
discoveries, and doing lots of good; and happily
he did no harm, except unto himself. Among
his lucid theories, was a grand one about spores,
as the protoplasm, or proto-phantasm, of all
sporadic existence. And his child appearing,
on the same day as his book, in spite of her
mother, he would have her name—" Sporetta."
Her name lasted longer than the book, because
it appealed to a larger audience, and nobody
could make out what it meant. But soon even
this sweet association vanished; for Sporetta
took the chicken-pox, before her skin was
hardened; and no hundred-headed Stentor, with
a high-pressure boiler, and three steam-whistles
in his every mouth, nay, nor even the foremost
statesman of the age, might ever have stormed
people's eyes, through their ears, to believe that

the child was not spotty. Her name had begun to be " Spotterer " already ; and now as the polystigmatic view deepened, her name accrusted finally to the positive form of " Spotty."

CHAPTER XI.

MOTHER DEAR.

WHEN two persons, as widely asunder in nature, as she ever lets us be, having long held imaginary notion of each other, for the first time come together in the bodily form, under stress of circumstance, what becomes of all they meant to do? Some men have had the happiness to see two dogs, who have been chained up, for some months of moonlight, within barking distance of each other, and having higher gifts than we possess, have appraised one another without interview, according as the wind blew to or fro—to behold these twain dogs meet upon the highway, at length and at last, for the very first time, on a day when there is wind enough to blow their tails off. Either dog has made his mind up, as to how he will behave; each knows every corner of his adversary's mouth, and which of his teeth has been broken by a bone; he has learned every item of his brother barker's story (from his howls to the man in the moon, to come and help him), and sitting on his haunches, he has fifty times rehearsed his proceedings with that noisy dog, when he shall come across him. Yet now, when the blissful opportunity is come, when the other dog is looking at him, smaller than his bark was, and easier to thrash than he ever has imagined him, does he fall upon, and rend him? No, not he; tails wag across the gale, with growing cordiality; sniffs try to baffle facts; good will is mutual; the weather is too bad, for any dog to say a word upon any other subject. In half a minute, they have managed to smell up a fundamental friend-ship; and henceforth, if they bark of nights, it will not be at, but with, each other.

Now Lady Touchwood, and Captain Larks, acted very differently from this. Their manner was as full of common sense, and of waiting for a leading question from each other, as Cæsar's, and Lion's, may be at first sight; but they failed of the insight, which man, (the only animal capable of envy), decries as instinct.

"I suppose this is the house of Captain Larks," said the lady in the little porch, looking at the owner, who had got his bridge down, and his door wide open. "Dr. Perperaps is with me. I am come to see my son, who has met with a very sad accident, I fear. Perhaps you are Captain Larks himself."

"I believe that I have the honour to bear that name," Mr. Arthur replied, with a very stiff bow; "at least in this part of the country. The boy is in no danger; but severely cut, and shaken."

"I suppose you will not refuse me liberty to see him. Perhaps in such a question, the very best judge is his mother." Lady Touchwood spoke sharply, and with what she took for irony.

"There is not any question in the case, that I am aware of. And there can be no question, as to your right to see him. Be careful, if you please; there is an awkward step here. Rose, my darling, Lady Touchwood will follow you. Hold your candle higher, that's a dear little child. My daughter, Lady Touchwood! Allow me to introduce her."

"Well!" communed the visitor, with her own heart only; "things must be come to a very pretty pass, when a man, who has run away from justice, and lives by selling pears, and apples, introduces his daughter to me, and orders me to follow her! And Mr. Short upbraids me with my quick temper! If he could see me now—— But never mind; they shall know my opinion of them, when Dicky can be moved."

In a very few minutes, however, Lady Touchwood began to waver largely, in her opinion of them; even as the tail of the inimical dog—whose "emotional condition" has been analysed above—unconsciously relaxes, from the wiry cock of defiance, first to the crisp bend of inquiry, then to the pleasing wave, of interest and sympathy, and lastly to the woolly wag, of amity, and brotherhood. So pervading is the tendency towards good will, in the breast of all genuine mammalia.

There could be no doubt, that much trouble had been taken, for the comfort and welfare of the adventurous rat-hunter: the motherly perception took this in, at a glance; and the deep sleep of the wounded one (which he suddenly accomplished) appealed to the tenderest, and most sacred feelings of maternity.

"Poor darling!" the mother whispered, having kissed his marble forehead; "how beautifully regular his breathing is! He always had that gift, whatever happened to him. Can I ever show my gratitude to heaven, Miss Larks, for the providential fact, that his features are uninjured? His features have been declared, by the first sculptor of the age, to be of the very purest classical ideal. Whether he said Doric, or Ionic, or perhaps Gothic, I will not be certain, at this exciting period."

"We made sure at first, that his nose was cut in two," replied Spotty Perperaps, who had done the lion's share, and would not be put in the background, like that; "but it turned out to be a stripe of red lead, my lady; and when I sponged it off, I found his dear nose all right."

"His dear nose, indeed! Who is this young female? Oh, the doctor's daughter, Spotty! Yes, I heard that you were here."

"And a good job for Master Dicky, that I came up with father," said the spirited Miss Perperaps, in a tone of self-assertion; "such little things as this always come into my compass."

The sturdy manner, and rather rough appearance of the damsel—too important as she was, to be affronted just now—brought into sweet contrast the gentle demeanour, and sympathising glances of the other young lady; who kept herself in the background, and then retired into the passage.

"Poor darling! Precious sufferer! I will disturb him no longer," Lady Touchwood whispered gently, as she tucked her Dicky's ears up. "Though it would have been such a rapture, to hear him even breathe my name. But heaven, in its wisdom, has sent this balmy slumber. Come forward, my dear; you are a very nice young lady. Miss Larks, I am pleased with you. Your behaviour is most becoming. You have never said a word, since I came in; though you cordially feel for me, in this sad affliction. Of course you are not a nurse, or anything of that kind. Miss Perperaps, who is so clever, and accustomed to it, will be quite indefatigable, I am sure, and will find me full of gratitude. But you, my dear, may also be of very great assistance to us; and I am certain, from your lovely eyes, that you are kind, and gentle."

Rose Arthur, being very shy with strangers, and reluctant always to be made conspicuous, came forward, just as far as manners, and her sense of obedience prescribed. There, the light of two candles (a gallant dip, and a lordly tallow-mould) combined to play upon her blushing cheeks, white forehead, and softly sparkling eyes. And strange to say, another pair of eyes (supposed to be buried in deep repose) contrived to unclose themselves, and steal a narrow glance, through glimmering lashes, as children " draw straws " from the fire.

" If I can be of any use," said Rose, " in any way whatever—I mean of course for messages, or outdoor work "—she qualified her offer, because she met the patient's eager gaze at her—" any little things, to save Miss Perperaps from—from coming away too much; I shall be very glad to be of use, I'm sure."

" I thought that I heard a heavy sigh,"— Lady Touchwood turned, as she spoke;—" surely our precious sufferer—— Dicky, dear, are you conscious of my presence, and pining for me ?"

A snore of the highest artistic order, superior to nature's sweetest effort, conveyed, to the mother's yearning heart, a solace at the same time, and yet a disappointment.

" I will suppress my very natural desire," she whispered to Rose, while Spotty turned away, and indulged in a broad grin, out of the window; " my fond wish to hear, if it were but a single syllable, from those dear lips. It is wrong, and selfish of me. How thankful should I be, for the balmy depth of this repose ! That is how he always sleeps, Miss Larks, ever since he fell and indented his ligaments, the day he was put into small clothes. I never quite understood what the process was; the result, however, has been remarkable. On no account let him be disturbed to-night, by so much as the mention of my name. He will not awake, for ten hours now. I know all his ways, so thoroughly. Sleep on, darling, and the angels be with you."

" You don't deserve to have such a ma," said Spotty, running up to her patient, as soon as his mother was out of ear-shot; " not to give her a kiss, or so much as a word ! "

" It is all very fine for you to talk," the youth replied, to soothe his conscience, by strong statement of his case; " you don't know any-thing at all about it. Do you suppose, that I could put up, with being cried over, and kissed, and cuddled, and called all sorts of nursery names, in the sight and hearing of—I mean while she—while other persons at least, who cannot be expected to know my proper age——— "

" Oh, indeed ! I see. To be sure ! " ex-claimed Miss Perperaps ; " you want to be taken for a man, before your time. You seem to have conceived an extraordinary affection, for somebody, instead of your mother. Lady Touchwood is talking with Captain Larks; now it will make her more happy, if I tell her all about it."

"If you do, I will tear every bandage off, and my death will lie at your door, Spotty. I have got an old watch, that I had at school; it is out of fashion now, but it goes very well; and I'll give it to you, if you only do your duty to me. People run you down, I know; but in my opinion, you are wonderfully clever."

"No, Master Dicky, I am not at all that. But I see a great many stupid things done by people, who ought to know better. Marrying again, for instance, and having other children; what do you think of that, Mr. Touchwood?"

"A man when he marries," said Dicky with solemnity, and hoping that somebody might be listening in the passage, "swears upon the Bible, to have only one wife, to cleave to her, to stick to her, to love, honour, and obey her. How can he do that, I should like to know, if he goes, and gets married to another woman? Besides, we are told, and I have to attend Divinity lectures, I assure you, that no man can be blameless, except he be the husband of one wife. And that is how I intend to conduct myself."

"How I wish that my pa," said Miss Per-peraps, with a sigh, "had attended Divinity lectures. But hush, Master Dicky, I can hear my lady going, and my dear papa is doing Dixon to her; you know what that means in our practice, I suppose?"

"No, I never heard of it. They don't show us things at Cambridge. Oh, Spotty, I do like you so, because you don't care!"

"But I do care. And that makes me see how things are. A Dixon is a swing-cask, a sort of water-barrow, a tub upon pins between two wheels, for going down the walks with. They have got one, in your father's place. They are all very well, while they stand at the pump, because there is a shore to them. But if you want to make them go, you have to be very careful. If you put too much in them, they kick up one way; and if you put too little, they kick up the other, and your trouble goes for nothing."

"I can understand that well enough," answered Dicky, whose mind was by no means of electric speed; "but what has it got to do, with the doctor, and my mother?"

"Everything," said Spotty, with a look of some contempt; "if my father were to make

too much of your injuries, he would terrify your
mother, and she would fetch a man from Exeter.
So the tub would go over, from having too much
in it. But if he made too little of your mishap,
why then it would be almost worse, for the tub
would go over the other way, because of being
empty."

" I wish you would talk plain English, Spotty.
All your stuff comes in bottles. What have
tubs got to do with it? But perhaps you make
enough to last the twelvemonth, at one brewing.
I can see what you mean, about another man
coming ; but I don't see what harm could come
of making little of it."

" Very well, if you can't see, you are not
worth telling. I would not have told you what
I have, only for the way in which they trampled
upon me. My dear pa is gone to see my lady
to her carriage, that wouldn't come up the hill,
because it is so rocky. Ah, I do admire Captain
Larks, for living where people must alight from
their chariots, to get at him."

" Spotty, you are a radical. I used to be one,
when I was very young, and could not see the
mischief of it. Wise people must be made to
leave it off. But politics always make me
sleepy. Go, and see whether my mother is clean

gone, and whether your father means to plague me any more. It shall never be said of me, that I made a fuss about a trifle. I dare say you would like to hear me groan. Girls always do; because then they can boast about having their teeth out, and all that, better than we men do. But I am as game, as a three-legged rat."

"Just you wait a bit, before you boast," Miss Perperaps answered, as she went to fetch her father; "your troubles are not begun yet, Master Dicky; the wound in your tibia has got some bull's-eye glass in it, and what is worse to my mind, green scum of rotten whiting. If you don't begin to squeak to-morrow, for certain you will, on Sunday."

CHAPTER XII.

" NOUS."

" THE idea is a good one.   Sometimes there is a
dove-tail to be made, of cross purposes, when laid
aright."   Mr. Short said this, to his well-beloved
Nous, as they sat down together, to consider
their breakfast and the business of the day, on
a very nice Monday morning.   Monday morning
is the sweetest of the week, not only for parsons,
but for dogs as well ; for they both have passed
through tribulation yesterday, and are all the
better for it ; and best of all, have six days
before them, ere the trial comes again.

Perhaps, it would be too wide a statement, to
aver that a parson is bound officially to feel a
depression of his bright, elastic, and naturally
large mind, and to get up at a low level, upon a
Sunday morning.   He means to preach admirably,
and he does it (often with some drain upon
his own resources) ; he has many sound ideas,

which he wants to watch, in their movement into wakeful minds ; and perhaps the very last of his desires is, to let anybody else come, and do it better for him. Still he is glad, and it is a proof of his humility to be so, when he has done his duty.

His dog, on the other hand, if tenderly attached to him—as a parson's dog is sure to be —rejoices with a treble bark, when the trying day is over. In the present " distracted condition of the church," he is not allowed to go there, though his clerical ancestors may have made a point of it. Sitting on the bricks, outside his kennel, he hears the fine call of the bells, and he smells the swing of the man, and the boy, who are ringing, because they both work in the vicarage garden. Then he sees a lot of people in the foot-path meadow (where a hare has a seat, to his certain knowledge, and a wedded pair of partridges come almost every evening) gingerly walking, with their best clothes on, and trying not to make too much noise, because they are getting near the church-yard. They have got a dog with them ; and his jealousy suggests, that a lay dog will be let in, where he is not. He quickens in his fore-legs, and gives a distant " wuff" at him, with a shake of his ears, and a toss of his nose, and a hope that he may know how to behave himself.

Then comes his final misery, the last straw that breaks his back. He has seen the two girls go, with their Sunday stripes, and flarings on, and their yellow cotton gloves, too fine for him to sniff at; also the boy who sweeps him up is gone—which was a pang to him, greater than that of petticoats—but when his master comes out the back way, locks the door, and hides the key in a clump of violets, and then with his sermon in the Spanish leather-case, scarcely vouchsafes him a one-handed pat, with a long reach, and a sidelong passage (because of his best black kersey), and is gone round the corner, with a flutter of his tails, too full of eloquence to talk to a dog—then he puts down his tail in the hole, he scratched advisedly, sits down, to keep down with it, and humbles all his arrogance, and the best-plumed portions of his very noble frame, by revolving on his haunches, with his nose up high supinely, and his heart appealing to his lungs, to come up with it in an unexampled howl.

Nous, having passed through all this anguish yesterday, as usual, was now in the highest of high spirits, this fine Monday morning. He

had heard his master order the horse *Trumpeter*
to be thoroughly well-fed, and ready for a long
ride, at half-past nine o'clock; and *Nous* had
ascertained, without putting one objectionable
question, that he was to go too. He had been
to the stable, and the kitchen, and the larder,
and several other places too; and all of these,
with one accord, announced that *Nous* was going.
If there had been any doubt about it, even at
the pessimistest moment, the quantity of really
fine victuals set before him was enough to con-
vince him most delightfully. "Lay you in a
broad, and good foundation for the day, my
friend," said his master to him; and it would
have been surplusage to repeat the order.

But apart from the question of nourishment,
however urgent and agreeable, this dog deserves,
and in his own right demands, consideration.
He was not one of those gigantic fellows, who
are patronized with some tender alarm concerning the issue, if they take it amiss; neither was
he one of those little whipper-snappers, whom it
is not worth while to propitiate. The first
question asked about a dog, by a man, is almost
sure to be an invidious, and rude one, and mainly
ungrammatical—"What breed is he?"

When John Sage of Christowell, who was

famous for shedding his own light on things, was told that a nobleman (too well known in that neighbourhood) was of very long descent, he shook his head, and said that he could understand it now. “ He hath not dooed it, of a zudden then,” said John; “ he hath a’ been coomin’ down, all that wai.” But *Nous*, though of long descent, was not come down like that; and the purity of his lineage shone forth in every lineament. A setter of generous birth was he, sable, distinguished with spots and gold, such as we men call “ black and tan;” flued, and feathered, and fringed with gold, so that while drawing on a covey up the gale, he resembled sombre night prolonged in pencils of Aurora. This may seem a rose-coloured picture of the dog, to those who have not the delight of looking at him, which really prevented some sportsmanlike artists from hitting the partridges, when they got up. Still even now, in his homelier moments, while begging for bacon, or chewing the rind (which seems to puzzle dogs’ teeth, more than tougher substance does), he deserved to be regarded, with eyes as attentive as his own, than which no more can well be said. For nothing was small enough to escape his eyes, or large enough to out-gauge them; but in his broad, calm pupils, all might be discovered, as in a lens, reposing, for him to think about. The clear depth of the rich brown iris spoke of contemplation, placid, and too profound for doubt, and a sensitive yearning to be praised, and patted. The loveliest lady in the land has not such eloquent, lucid, loving eyes; and even if she had, they would be as nothing, without the tan spot over them. Neither might any lady vie with him, for accuracy, length, and velvet texture, and delicately saline humidity of nose.

"*Nous,*" said his master, whose thoughts were quick enough for one of our race, but very slow against a dog's, " things have turned out very pleasantly for us. If I had been obliged to go on Saturday, I should have doubted about taking you, because I must have meditated over my sermon, and you are a distracting animal. If you come across grouse on the hills, or even a snipe, or a plover, you insist upon working the question out, without any regard for their connubial state. But now upon a Monday, I am as free as you are. You shall enjoy yourself; and so will I."

For the vehement lady herself had called, upon her return from the " scene of probation "

—meaning Mr. Arthur's cottage—and begged the good vicar to put off his trip; for she could not think twice about the wilful Julia, while her dear obedient boy lay on a bed of suffering, through his self-sacrificing heroism. Oh, if it only had been Julia, she said, it would have been so much nicer then, to recognize the hand of Providence! Mr. Short smiled dryly, and revolved in his mind some rumour that had reached him, concerning bottled beer. But he gladly put off his long ride, till the Monday, and paid a short visit, on Saturday, to the interesting Dicky, who was now shedding salt tears into water-gruel, and gazing at three bottles, hatted with pill-boxes, and booted to the knees with slimy sediment. Spotty stood before him, and he knew that words were vain, and the deepest sigh would be no more than a signal for a gargle.

Now, Mr. Short loved both his horse, and his dog; and to see them thus full of the joy of the outbreak, from stable and kennel, and the glory of the air, and the hope of adventure, and distinction, and renown, was sure to set his own spirit capering with theirs, and the dark soul of man flitting into sunny places, and even the mind soaring into the air, out of which it was taken, and to which it shall return. The air was more delightful than the mind to-day; and to ride was far better than to reason.

"Halloa, *Nous*, you should have done your pranks by this time," the master shouted to him, as the dog stood still, suddenly, amazedly, and with a headlong point; as a young dog, rashly scouring, does too late, when he is almost on the tails of game; "an old stager, like you, should know better than that. No birds can be here; yet you never stand a lark. A hare on her form, no doubt of it. Down wind on a hare, with his nose upon her back. *Nous* would stay there all day; I must go up, and see."

It is a fine, and ardent sight, to see a noble dog, ranging as freely as the wind, check his long stride, stand still, and stiffen, with his fore feet planted upon the advance, his arched loins straightened into a hard strung line, his head (that was tossing on high just now) levelled, and rigid as an anvil's nose; his upper lip quivering, despite his iron will, and the fixed eyes labouring to learn from their own whites, whether the master is hurrying up to shoot. Meanwhile the hare—for a bird very seldom abides to be considered so intently—crouches into the closest compass, with every sinew on the spring, yet still; and suppressing every ruffle of her gingery fluff, lowers the lids of her soft bright eyes, for fear of a sparkle through the russet of her flax; while she watches every hair's breadth of her enemy, and hopes that nobody has seen her.

Expecting to rejoice in this well-known sight, and the blissful bound of the unchased hare, when the dog lies down, and never stirs an inch, but bedews the ground from the fountain of his mouth, the vicar turned *Trumpeter's* head, and rode up, to release the good dog from his statuary state. " Toho, *Nous!* " he said, just to keep up the tradition; though the dog was too wise to want admonition. But to his surprise, a great change came over the spirit of the animal, and his body also, ere ever the horse's hoofs were nigh. The first sign of weakness was a flutter of the tail, a delicate tremor of the golden brush, in which an artistic dog concludes. Then the firm line of the back relaxed, the curved ears fell, and the countenance looked foolish; and after a feeble sniff, or two, the whole dog set off helter skelter, down the dingle, at whose head he had been standing, like a statue. There was no hare before him;

neither anything moving, in the long desolation, except himself.

"Now, this is to my mind a horrible puzzle," the vicar exclaimed, as he pulled up at the spot, where the false point had so long held good; "*Nous* never chases fur, or feather; and if he did, there is none to be chased. He has made a thorough fool of himself for once. But no, I beg his pardon. There has been some scamp here, and he has killed a sheep, I see! Come back, come back, my darling, or you will get a knife stuck into you."

In an agony of dread, for he loved his dog most dearly, and the rocky dell forbade all hope of riding to his succour, he put his nails between his lips, and gave a long shrill whistle; and the dog's obedience saved his life. In the distance, down at the end of the combe, a pale blue mist overhung a morass, in which a little stream lost itself. *Nous*, in full gallop down the grass-track, stopped short at the whistle, with a big stone just beside him, and a heavy charge of duck-shot scattered peat, and moss, around him. But the big stone had sheltered him, and not a hair was hurt of him, while the roar of the gun rang up the hollow, and the smoke of strong powder spread a dirty blur before the clean blue mist. From the mixture of vapours, a figure with a long gun strode forth rapidly, to bag poor *Nous;* but he, with his innocent tail between his legs, and a deep (but brief) sympathy for creatures that are shot at, was swallowing the hard ground, best foot foremost, by the way that he came, and thanking his stars to be rid of a rogue, and to see his good master.

If ever, in the history of the church, any parson has been unfitted by his own “ emotions ” —which is now become the proper English name of wrath, shame, desire, revenge, and other good and bad feelings—for delivering with emphasis one short, and strong commandment, and thoroughly fitted for the breach of that same, that man was now Vicar of Christowell. Saddened, and cowed by the narrow escape, which had shaken his faith in humanity (because he understood a gun so well, and took such pleasure in its proceedings, when it shot at the proper animals), *Nous* lay down, before *Trumpeter's* feet, and panted, and looked very piteously up; for his self-esteem held two deep wounds, of the false point, and of being fired at.

Having been at Winchester, and New College (seats of the Muses, where they are so much at home, that their language is not always foreign),

Parson Short used a short word; who shall heed what it was, if it bettered his philanthropy? Then he jumped from his horse, and bent over the dog, in quick fear of finding some big shot-hole; so sad were his favourite's attitude, and gaze.

Like every other creature, this dog most heartily loathed examination, and strove to escape it, by offering paws, and by putting up his nose, as no candidate can do.

"You old humbug, you are not hurt a bit. All that you want is, to be made much of; because you have made such a fool of yourself. Hi, find!—fetch—drop! Now you are yourself again. Let us see, what there has been here, to make such a mighty fuss about."

Nous, having flipped in, and out of, the heather, after his master's glove, and brought it, with the greater agility of the canine mind, had recovered his balance, and was equal to his duties. With his valuable nose, he described exactly the outline of the form, which he had taken for a hare's, and dwelled more especially upon those spots, which retained the warmest impression of the shape we so admire. "He had no more than two legs,"—*Nous* pronounced as he smelled him out—"and two things here,

that you call arms; and he lay upon his back,
and he had no tail. And my opinion of him is,
that he was very dirty."

" Never mind; it is no use to think any more
about it," Mr. Short replied, as his manner was,
to his dog's observations ; " there is no getting
near the fellow, be he who he may. And since he
has not hit you, my good *Nous*, I have chiefly
to regret, that the arch-enemy was so sharp, as
to take advantage of my anxiety about you."

Thus, in a comparatively thankful mood, these
two went upon their way together ; for the
nature of the ground forbade all hope of pur-
suing the hang-dog skulker. But Mr. Short
felt that his spirits were dashed, and docked of
their bright April flow, by such a nasty out-
rage, within five miles of his own warm, and
hospitable roof.   His character was well known,
and valued, all over the eastern side of the moor,
among the few people, who dwelled, or wandered
there.   Not a whit less known was the character
of *Nous*, wherever there was any heart capable
of valuing integrity, docility, gallantry, and
faith.   No moorman would ever dream " of
letting off his gun "—as they always express
it—at Parson Short's *Nous*; even if he had a
gun, which was not a common thing with them.

It must be some fellow, of the outlaw sort, was the only conclusion Mr. Short could form —such as came harbouring, and harassing most grievously, treading the loose foot-prints of the Gubbins' family, striking every traveller with terror, and dismaying all quiet people, round the verges of the waste. The great Castle-prison, in which all the sadness of the long moor culminates, was empty at this time, and faced the sunshine—whenever there was any—with peaceful moss. Neither warrior, nor felon, could have crept from out its gloom, to crouch in the bog by day, and prowl among the sheep at night.

However, Mr. Short, possessing that invaluable gift, a sweet and happy mind, rode on; and a league, or two, of moorland breeze, in trackless space, where distant tors are the traveller's direction-posts, began to make him feel, how small, and ludicrous is human wrath. His course lay, as nearly as might be, north-west, over some of the highest land of Dartmoor; for his old friend's house, which he had not yet seen, stood below the north-western parapet of highland, two, or three, miles to the south-west of Okehampton, and a little way back from the Tavistock road. Well as he knew his own side of the moor, he was taken aback by some pieces of travel, which he met between Yes-tor and Cranmere pool; but hitting the West Ockment, near Black-tor, he contrived to get down to Okehampton Park.

On the Tavistock road, which he was truly glad to reach, he saw, as he rode up the bank from the river, a young man walking briskly, with a handsome setter-pup, about six months old, and of white and lemon colour, with legs, and tail, as yet unfringed. The motto of *Nous*, as of all dogs then, was "*canis sum, nihil canini,*" &c.; and therefore up he ran, though his bronzy toes were becoming rather sore, to pass the time of day, to this young member of his race. The white and lemon animal saluted him, as was decent, and then kindly submitted to further olfaction, lowering his tail, in token of communion with his elder, with a dog of dignity, and established position in the world. *Nous* was naturally pleased with this, although it is the duty which all pups render—if they desire to grow on into tax-payers—and he pleasantly allowed the adolescent dog to skip, and vault around him; while he wagged his own tail slightly, and sniffed, with a critical air, at the salutation offered. Then the dog of experience

warned the pup, that he had said his say, and
been accepted with indulgence, and must consider this interview closed, unless he were prepared to have tooth, instead of tongue. *Nous*
was very seldom crusty; but to be shot at, and
to jog along for hours, without seeing game,
and to get raw toes, tries even a dog's philosophy.

"I take leave to apologize, for my dog's
growls," said Mr. Short, riding up with *Trumpeter*, who shook his legs out, as he felt them
on a tidy road once more; "but he will not
hurt your young dog, sir."

"Thank you; I am not afraid of that,"
replied the other; "I was only looking at your
dog, because I like them; and he seems a very
fine one."

"He is a very fine one, and not to be
matched, I believe, in the four counties. But
will you kindly tell me, where Colonel Westcombe lives? It must be somewhere about
here."

"Not more than a mile; and I am going
straight home. You have ridden far to-day, sir,
and come across the moor. My father has long
been hoping to see an old friend—Mr. Short, of
Christowell."

"I am the man; and you are young Jack

Westcombe; or at least you ought to be, because there is no other." The vicar was so pleased to see his old friend's son, and to find him to his liking, that he shaped his sentence anyhow, got off his horse, and took him by both hands, and examined him, as carefully as if he were a nag, whose price he meant to have £5 off.

Knowing that he meant him well, and was not trying to abate him, Jack Westcombe looked him in the face, with a shy, but pleasant expression, and a twinkle of goodwill.

Then the vicar said, " Yes, you are the image of your father; only taller, and slighter, and your nose is straighter; and you look as if you stood upon your own rights more. I fear, you will never be quite equal to him. That, of course, is not to be expected. Still, you may do well enough, for the rising generation. We don't expect the young dogs to come up to the old ones. But march on, and let me have a good look at you. You are like your father, in one thing, and that a very great one—you don't want to talk too fast, young Master Jack."

The young man, smiling at the short ways of the parson, did as he was ordered; *Trumpeter*, being gifted with a Roman nose, tossed it, and made good his name, by a lively blare to some large stables, which he espied in the distance, and hoped to flourish there in, a stall, and a store *non ignobilis otî*.   In reply, the rooks began to caw, the queists to flit out of the ivied elms, the little dog, and the big dog, to yelp and bay, respectively, the gardener (who was resting on his laurels) to get up, the young lady, reading in a snaily chair, to gaze about; and all the other things began to embrace the rare opportunity of saluting a new arrival, at an ancient country-house.

CHAPTER XIII.

OLD FRIENDS, AND YOUNG ONES.

SHELTERED from the west winds, by the first of the range of hills, that trend away towards Cornwall, and from the east, by Dartmoor, Westcombe Hall is as nice a place, as any lover of a samely life, and a changeful landscape, may desire. For the beauty of the hills is variety of rigour, and the beauty of the valley is variety of softness; and the comfort of the home-life, is to see them, and be steadfast. Colonel Westcombe entered into such things calmly, without any consideration of them, after the battle of life, he had been through.

The cawing of the rooks was a settled pleasure to him, and the lowing of the distant cows a space of soothing interest; the trees, and all the garden-plants (of which he had small knowledge) excited him to think about them, from the sense of ownership; and he began to study cocks, and hens, without any skewers through them. For still he was as lively as ever he had been ; and the quantity of carnage, he had smelled in fields of glory, acquitted these, his elder days, of the younger duty to destroy.

"Short, you see those trees," he said, as he sauntered forth, with that old friend, after dining at the old-fashioned hour, five o'clock ; "wait a moment, come in here ; never mind the young folk, they will get on well enough ; though I don't want Jack to have her. Now here we can have a delicious little smoke. You like a pipe, so do I ; not cigars—I have seen too much of the way they make them. Very well ; help yourself. How very glad I am to see you !" This was the fiftieth time of saying that ; but the parson said, "And so am I," very nearly every time. "You see those trees there," continued Colonel Westcombe, leaning back in his bower arm-chair ; "they are a little green with moss, and so on—soft to the eye, I should call it, Short."

"It is the duty of a tree to be as green as possible ;" Mr. Short answered, with a puff of blue smoke.

"You always cut my corners off. I mean, that the trunks of the trees are green ; and that is not their duty. Well, this fellow, who is considered, and may be, the shining light of the neighbourhood, counselled me to peel off all the green, and treat the fine old fellows to three coats of whitewash. A pleasant view we should have had, from the windows, all the summer! What do you say to that? You know everything."

"Do I? I don't know that, to begin with. The extent of my knowledge is, to know how much I don't know; for which I heartily thank Oxford. But I do know a man, who understands such things, and could give you the very best advice. Or rather I mean,—he is not to be had now; no, no, we must not think of him."

"That reminds me," his host replied, "of the wonderful fellow in your parish, Short. A gentleman, you say he is; and you are no bad judge. You held out some hopes, that we might see his place; and what would please me even more, see him. You know that I am foolish, as my nature is, about things that come up, and take my fancy. I don't want to spend a lot of cash, of course; nobody ever does; and how can I tell, that I may not be turned out again, neck and crop? Another will might be dis-

covered; or what not? And I am not sure that
I should lament it very much. I like to do
things for myself; and I believe every man
under Wellington got into that style. We had
no fine gentlemen, I can tell you ; none of your
Pompey's officers. But no more of that—you
have heard it too often. All I meant to say is,
that I want to get this place into a little better
order ; partly, because I like to see things
decent, and partly because the people round
about are not very well off; and yet to offer
them money, except as wages, is an insult."

This was a very long piece of discourse, for
Colonel Westcombe to get through, without
stopping ; although he could tell a long story
pretty well, when he thought it his duty, and got
a good start. Meanwhile, Mr. Short was in a
sad dilemma, (although he had foreseen this, and
rehearsed it long) between his warm frankness
to his old friend, and his duty, and goodwill, to
that one living in his own dear parish. But he
settled aright, and against his own desire—
which is one of the true tests of right decision
—to leave the captain dark as ever, in his own
recess, and to stave off the colonel's curiosity
about him. To the former, it might be a matter
of great moment ; whereas it is very little loss to

any man, to be robbed of a thing that he never uses, unless he has paid for it heavily—advice.

"You ought to begin at once, if you mean to do much good," said the vicar, looking round at the overhung lawn, and the trees moustached with moss, and fungus; "you are six weeks later, on this side of the moor, than we are at Christowell. But even here, not a day is to be lost, if you mean to do planting. My friend cannot possibly leave home now; and an accident has happened (a very sad affair, of which you will hear by-and-by) not on his threshold, but much worse—through the roof of his favourite vinery. I would not spoil your dinner, and some other little doings, by making your dear godchild anxious. And in reason, there need not be a shadow of anxiety, except for those wondrous doctors. Old Betty Sage, John Sage's Betty, would have put Dicky Touchwood on his pins in three days, with her simples, and careful diet. But our Dr. Perperaps, a truly fine practitioner, and a man of solid grounding, will scarcely get him out of hand, within three weeks, and may have to make three months of it."

"What has happened to poor Dicky then? And why is Julia not to know?" The colonel gave a short, quick puff of smoke, because he hated mystery.

"There is no mystery at all about it," replied Mr. Short, who had his own turn of temper, and knew every nerve of his old friend's mind; "Dicky Touchwood tumbled through the roof of a greenhouse, or vinery, or something—I don't understand their distinctions—and he cut his legs, or what he calls his legs, as much as such nonentities could well be cut. He came down, like a tipsy-cake stuck with splinters; and tipsy he was, unless they told me lies. But our place is not to jeer, but sympathize. I have not ventured into this short narrative, till now, because one can never tell, how anything will act upon another mind, or at any rate, a female one."

"Short, you are right. I have observed that, often. The women know best in the end, I believe; but you never can tell, how they know it. Julia is full of sense; wonderfully so, to my mind; she gets at almost anything, five minutes before I do; and she sticks to it too; and that proves that she is right. But between you, and me, and the bedpost, Short—as the old ladies say—I don't want Jack to have her. There could not be a better girl, in many ways of looking at her. But she must have her own way, although she gets it gently. Jack, on the other hand, is very easy-tempered; but turn him you cannot, when once he has made his mind up. His wife, when he is old enough to want one, which we never used to think of, when I was young, should be amiable, gentle, . fond of little jokes, and capable of making them when he wants them, well-bred, and totally indifferent about dress—the new fashions, I mean, and all that rubbish, that some women study, more than their own behaviour—also she ought to be diligent, and thrifty, tidy, and particular to keep him to his meal-times, an experienced judge of meat, and butter, full of understanding about doors, and windows, thoroughly warm-hearted, and not inclined to cough, when she smells tobacco-smoke."

"To think of such a wife, makes a man's mouth water," Mr. Short answered, with a serious look; "there used to be some of them; but the young women now think more of themselves, than of anything else. It is my place, to pay attention to the women—well, not in the way that you are smiling at, my friend—what I mean to say is——"

"Well done, Short!" cried the colonel, putting down his pipe, and laughing heartily; "well done, my dear fellow! To be sure it is. And you magnify your office. I shall tell my dear wife that."

"Now don't you be too clever; but just hear me out. A parson must attend to his women, not only for their own sake, but also to get at the men. You understand all about regiments, and that; but you never even heard perhaps of 'parish work.' It is almost a new idea, in the Church as yet; and I am not at all sure, that it will do much good, because it comes from the Dissenters, I believe. If we come to make a fuss of it, it will do a lot of harm, and make our flocks take it into their heads, that our object is to drive them. They like very much to be driven, by fellows they can turn out, as soon as they are tired of them; but they never will be driven by a gentleman; so that all these doings must be done with skill."

"I don't like to hear of such absurd inventions. When I was a boy, I knew a good deal of the clergy; and in Spain I came across some priests, who were very good and holy. But to come back to the women, Short—you understand them, do you?"

"No, I never said anything to that effect.

Only, that I have to study them; which is a different thing altogether. You were talking about Miss Touchwood, and the sort of wife your son should have. I know the very girl for him —such a beauty—and a first-rate gardener; as well as all that you require. But two people cannot be matched by pattern. I have made a lot of matrimony, fetching them up to it, when it was needful, and reading the bans, and going through with it; and unless there is very bad temper on both sides, they get on respectably afterwards. But I am talking horn-book."

"Horn-book ought to be talked much more, in the present wild days," said the colonel. " Soon there will be nothing sacred. Every idiot laughs at institution. However, to come back to Julia. She is a very handsome girl; and Jack—well, I don't want her to be too much here. She came to us suddenly; I don't-know why; but rather out of spirits, and I could not ask the reason. My dear wife, who might have got it out of her quite prettily, has been laid up all the while, with a very bad attack; but she told me, in confidence, that it ought to be a love-affair."

" Rather the contrary," answered the parson ; " but as she has not told you, I will not. Her mother was unkind to her, to put it mildly. You know that 'my lady'—as she loves to be called—is sometimes very prompt of action. However, there are worse people in the world; and I trust that they are burning to be reconciled. I brought as good a message to Miss Touchwood, from her mother, as could be expected, considering their relation. Also I said, that poor Dicky wanted her; and she promised to go home to-morrow."

"Short, you are a public benefactor. Three cheers for the influence of the clergy. I shall be sorry to lose Julia, of course; but still I would rather lose her, than Jack. Young fellows, nowadays, think very little of the wisdom of their parents. But who is the girl, that he ought to have? I shall come, and see her, if she lives at Christowell."

"Time enough to think of that, my friend. No one admitted, except on business. You will have to send your card in, and write upon it, 'I want to see the young lady, Jack ought to have.' But what a hurry you are in, about him! He is only three-and-twenty, according to my reckoning. 'Let un 'baide,' as John Sage says, 'let un 'baide, till a' getteth a buzzum.' By-the-by, our John would suit you well, for laying out ground, or for seeing to your trees, or shaping out a new kitchen-garden. All flowers he despises, except cauliflowers. He says that the Lord made the flowers to grow wild, on purpose to vex Solomon; but Solomon, and the Lord together, couldn't grow cabbage, without manure—or 'mannering,' as he calls it. He knows the Old Testament, ten times as well as I do."

"Short, I will have him; if only for that. Such men are obstinate; but brave, and honest. I have seen lots of them, in the army, generally Scotchmen. No infidel Frenchman could stand before them. How much money will he want, a week?"

"Eight shillings is the proper thing at Christowell. But then they get pickings, that work it up to nine, and even ten, in harvest-time. But I am not at all sure, that he would go from home. Our people know, when they are well off."

"Let him come to me, for three months, and go home for the harvest. I will give him twelve shillings a week, and house-room. And if we get on together, he may settle here."

"Tell it not, on our side of the moor; and warn him, not to speak of it. Every solid head in our parish would be turned; but Sage can keep his own counsel. He shall come to you, by this day week; but only on a three months' lease, at the longest. Christowell will not be itself, without him; and if anything important comes to pass, we shall have to send for him, to pronounce upon it. I shall miss him in church, more than a big pewful; he nods at me always, when I say the right thing, and he taps on the floor, with his ground-ash stick."

"We will not rob you of such a hearer, Short," said the colonel, perceiving what a sacrifice he asked; "your church, and parish, shall enjoy him, on a Sunday. I told you that I had taken, from the Duchy, a lease of the sporting over some ten thousand acres, upon which there may be ten head of game, in a favourable season. But, at £10 a year, it is cheap enough; and I may improve it, if I can. It was done through my old friend, General Punk, who has interest with the steward, and who promised to come down, every year, if I would do it; and it is cheap enough to see an old friend, at that rent. And Jack was quite up for it, when I told him; for he likes to march forty miles a day, I do believe; which is all very well, when you choose for yourself your route, your weather, and your toggery. I intend to try red grouse there, as well as black. They do in bleaker places than Dartmoor even. It is not a new experiment—I know that. But experiments require luck, and perseverance, even more than skill, I do believe. At any rate, I mean to try it."

"You are a sanguine man," the vicar answered; "I wish that I could say so, of myself. But try it, my dear fellow; by all means, try it. But John Sage does not understand game-keeping."

"And I don't want him to understand it," returned the gallant colonel; "it is not like pheasant-hatching, or skilled work. You turn out your grouse, with their wings a little tipped, and you let them take their chance; that is my idea. Only they must not be harassed, just at first, until they learn their whereabouts; or off they go. And it must be done, at the right time of year, and according to the season. Some of my birds are turned out already. Another batch comes next week; and failing these, I shall try a lot of cheepers, in June, if I can get them. You know that I am not a strict game-preserver. I would never insist upon 'pheasants v. peasants' —as the radical papers term it. But my little crotchet can breed no ill-will; for everybody about here is delighted with it; and it will put money in some honest fellow's pocket."

"But how will John Sage help, in this little scheme?   He may be the wisest of mankind, as everybody knows, and especially himself—but he doesn't know a grouse from a game-cock, or at any rate, not a red one."

"So much the better.   He will take more interest in the subject, from its novelty.   But have no fear, Short, of my perverting your Solomon, into a Nimrod.   Nothing of the kind is in my thoughts.   My grouse hobby only concerns him thus—I have made a little hut in the shelter of a tor—I think they call it Weist-tor, but I never know their tors—where a man may be comfortable, and put up his pony.   I want an honest man to be there, every now and then; or to have it supposed, that he may be there.   It is about half way, to your delightful parish; which seems to be the home of every virtue.   Very well; Sage shall have the old grey pony, who knows every stone upon the moor, I do believe; and every Saturday, if he likes to do it, he shall set off for his native place, with a gallon of cider, and a bag of kitchen-victuals, and be his own master till Monday morning."

"It is well discovered, and it shall come true,"

Mr. Short answered, with a smile at thinking of the figure Sage would cut, and the importance he would show; " the old man understands the moors, as well as a pee-wit; and better than your red grouse will. But one thing you forget— the superstition of the race. Weist-tor is almost as awful, to the native mind, as Wistman's wood, or even Cranmere pool itself. If you gave John Sage £10 every time, he would not go there at night-fall."

" We will get over that, somehow, or other. Entrap him there once, and he will grow foolhardy. I can always make men go, where I want to send them. I have set my mind on this, because it will keep up regular communication between us. I shall send you butter, and grapes, when I get any; and you can send me, now and then, a comb of the honey, for which Christowell is famous. You get about half the rain, that we do, I believe. But what a time Manx is, with our coffee! I must go and rout him up, I do believe."

" Here comes our coffee; well done, cup-bearer! The best, and the cleverest dog, in the world. No, not to me first; to the colonel first, because, though I am the visitor, you are my butler. That's right. Did you see, my dear fellow, how he balanced it?"

"Talk about reasoning powers!" said the colonel; "I never saw any man do it, half so well. And this is your dog, *Nous*, then? I am not given to envy; but—my goodness—did you notice how he wagged his tail? He would not do it, till you took the cup, for fear of spilling. Well, I have seen the very best-bred footman laugh, at a joke of his betters (as they call themselves), and spoil a lady's dress, while she was putting in her cream. And they talk of these dogs having no mind, Short!"

"Not only does *Nous* understand plain English," answered Mr. Short, as the dog laid down the little butter tub, which had contained the cups, "but he knows what is passing in a man's mind, better, very often, than the man himself does. But women are a dreadful puzzle to him."

"So they ought to be; I admire him the more. Come here, and let me thank you, good dog, and clever one. Short, you are too sharp for me. I never even knew this dog was here. You arranged it all with Manx, as to what he was to do."

"Not a bit of it. I told the man, that he could wait at table; but he laughed at me; and thus is he discomfited. I told your stableman, when he knotted *Nous* up, that no knot known in the Royal Navy would hold the dog, more than two hours; but he laughed, and said that unless he bit the rope through, he was fast for ever. He never attempts to bite any rope now, because I smacked him for it, once; but he unties any knot, with nose, tongue, and foot."

"It has made your poor nose bleed, old doggie; show us what it is then? You mustn't be so clever." Colonel Westcombe loved dogs; and they always felt it.

"It must be something else. Upon my word, the wretch has hit him. Just a graze on the tip of his sensitive nose; and his labour at the knot has set it off."

Then the vicar, in hot indignation, poured forth his grievance against that low skulk with a gun, which he had not spoken of at dinner-time, for fear of spoiling cheerfulness. His host listened gravely, and was shocked at such low villainy; and said that he had heard of a desperate fellow, lurking in the depths of the moor, and killing sheep; and the moor-men were afraid of him, because he had a gun.

"Sooner, or later, we shall catch him," he continued; "I have heard of him, from our chief constable. He believes him to be a noted murderer; a fellow who has killed two women, in cold blood. Let us say no more about him. Do you see Julia? How noble she looks, when her spirit is up! Master Jack has got more than he can do, to hold his own."

With the pair in the distance, who had no coffee, things were going on, even as he said. Jack Westcombe, although he had taken his degree, or perhaps for that reason, was shy with young ladies; of whom he knew little, having never a sister, to lead him amongst them, and describe their little tricks. Miss Touchwood knew this, and made the most of it.

"Do you mean to say, Mr. Westcombe," she went on; "that you mean to do nothing, and be nothing, in the world? It does seem such a waste of power, in these very earnest times."

"My great aunt was asking me about it the other day," said Jack, who had a dry way, when heavily attacked, of remitting his assailants to their own business; "and she has a right to ask, because she means to leave me something."

"Yes, to be sure; how good of her! She must have entered into the more recent spirit, the glorious development of mind, and matter. What a joy it is, to find that these high perceptions are penetrating, even to the passing generation! What an incentive to the younger mind! Did she propose any definite work, anything earnest, and advancing?"

"She did; an advance very definite indeed; but scarcely of a nature, perhaps, to interest young ladies. I will tell Lady Touchwood of it, when I come over."

"My mother takes very little interest in improvement. She seems to think it quite enough, to be no worse than we used to be."

"But your brother, Miss Touchwood; surely he may be developed, elevated, rendered progressive, and all that?"

"Unfortunately, my brother has no mind," she replied, with firm serenity; "but many people seem to like him all the better for it; particularly, I believe, at Cambridge. But you are very different. Your father has been telling me, how much he is afraid that you will be too intellectual."

"My father is the kindest-hearted man, in all the world. And since he came into this property, he thinks it his very first duty to be cheated, right and left; especially by his very intellectual son."

"How I admire this grand old place!" the young lady cried, as she sprang upon a bank of moss, besieged with primroses; " any one, who lives here, ought to be cheated; just to balance nature's gifts. Look, how the sunset warms, and deepens, the crimson of the bricks, and the grey granite facings, and the glitter of the ivy round the bows! And the grand old trees, full of mystery, and honour; and the beautiful slope of the lawn, unbroken by patches of glaring ugly dazzle, and patterns of hideous stiffness; and the murmur of the brook, like a soft strain of music, coming through the joyful buds of spring. Oh, how I wish our place was like this!"

" I have never been at Touchwood Park," said Jack, looking slyly at his beautiful companion, whose colour was heightened, and figure set forth, by excitement; " but from all, that I hear, it is a brilliant place, one of the highest developments of the age. This is a very old, humdrum, benighted, obsolete product of the darker ages. I am sure, you would never like to live here."

" Wouldn't I? If I only had the chance!" Then Julia blushed deeply, as her eyes met his; and even Jack's cheeks, which were always rather ruddy, showed sympathy with the sunset, as the fair one turned away.

CHAPTER XIV.

A SMALL COMMISSION.

Upon the dreary moor, there is little pleasure
of spring, or joy of summer; because of the
absence of that beauty (transcending the loveliest daughter of mankind), the excellent beauty
of the trees; which man was meant to nourish,
but loves better to demolish.

Only in the softer wrinkles, where the hard
face of the land relaxes into a smile aside, has
any tree a hope of standing, against the fierce
wind, and scowling sky. But in the few spots,
where shelter helps them, and frugal virtue of
the soil gives food, the pleasure of surprise
multiplies their beauty; and the jagged granite
sets their green off, with a spiked white chain
around their necks. These quiet dingles are
the very sweetest places, for any man to wander
through, with the spring of the year around

him, and the sound of crispness following his steps, and plenty of time to see things grow.

When the smiting wind, from the wilderness, leaps over the bristly ramp of furze, and after a few dying kicks, expires; the soft kind creatures, that have finer feelings, rejoice down below, and hug themselves. For here, they have safety, and comfort, and repose, and a soil glad with sweet ooziness; and the sprinkle of tempestuous air ruffles through them peacefully, and the hushing of the wind is music.

In such a gentle place, set largely with promiscuous hope, and strewn with more than good intentions of the modest work of spring, the foot of a savage man crushed the moss, and a tumult, harsher than that of the wildest wind, stirred through the branches. Forsaken of all his fellows' love, and disdainful of his Maker's, as wild a man as ever trod the earth; because he had no love of anything. Even as a baby of low nature may be known, by its cruel look at a little bird, or fly, and a boy of nasty instincts, by his torture of a frog; so a thoroughly hard man shows himself, by doing despite to the goodwill of his mother earth.

This man came along, with a fierce glitter in his eyes, and a slouching of his lumpy neck, and scorn of men stamped upon his bulky forehead, gingery brows, and grimy cheeks. The shape of his face had once been fine, the features strong, and regular; and a mighty strength of will had made it, in the prosperous days, impressive. But no one would think of considering it now, as a matter of kind interest; the impulse, of any one beholding it, would be to prefer the other side of Dartmoor.

The man, who was tall, and of vigorous frame, contrived to crush everything, that could be crushed by one pair of feet, planted recklessly. His coat was of undressed sheepskin, with the wool torn, and worn, by the briars, and rocks; his breeches were of rickcloth, sewn roughly by himself; his cap of badger-skin; and about him there was nothing of tradesman's work, except his boots. These had been stolen, from a shop, or cart, or perhaps from some gentleman's dwelling-house; for clearly enough, they were boots of good art, flexible, shapely, strong, and lively, and really inclined to be waterproof, on the feet of a clever wearer. They had a very clever wearer now, who, instead of cracking them with blacking, anointed them daily with raw fat, which they sucked into their constitution.

There were many who desired to catch this man, for a heavy reward was upon him; but any one, looking at him, would think twice, before raising hand, to lay hold of him. For he carried a big double-barrelled gun, of heavy bore, not too long to be handy, and having percussion locks, a novelty as yet among the simple sportsmen of the moor. Wild, and savage, and reckless as he looked, with the stain of the bogs, and the fray of the rocks, and ravellings of time, and weather; it was manifest, that he set store by his gun, which was clean, well-oiled, and in good condition. Even now, fiercely as he trod his way, among delicate growth, frail bud, and gentle flower, he bore his heavy weapon carefully, and watchfully, lest any bough should bruise, or sharp rock scratch it. Also he kept his keen eyes on the strain, for he was going to a doubtful, and perilous appointment.

" If he has doubled on me, he dies first," was the comfort he kept on administering to himself, although it did not make him comfortable; " he would turn upon himself, if he were paid, and could run away from it. There are many blackguards in the world; but none fit to hold a candle, to my clever, and exalted friend. He has thriven, and I have failed; because I had scruples, and he had none. But I have one pull upon him—his life is much to him; mine is a very small thing to me."

In the bend of this glen, where the wood grows thickest, there is a little driblet of a spring, that falls—by way of an early lesson to itself—almost as soon as it has done rising, over a rib of its hard mother granite. Certainly a few things fond of water come to alleviate its first mishap—moss for instance, and the stems of wet-bine, and crinkled caddis reeds, that introduce themselves, as conduits. Still there the fall is, and it must be fallen, even though it be five bad yards deep, amid a little jubilee of fluttering expectants, flower, and leaf, and crocketed frond, jerk-tailed gnat, and snub-nosed fernweb, the little mouse that lives in a gossamer almost, and the rabbit who builds him a castle of sand—all of them rejoicing in the tiny spout of crystal, the jeopardy of a sprinkle, from a whiff of wind across it, and the freshness of the seed-pearls, that glisten in the sunshine, or make a sliding string of some long flower-stem they have stolen.

Upon a slab of granite, near a stool of budding hazel, where the clear little thread of water frayed itself into a fantastic knot, at the base of the crag that shaped it, there sat a man of impatient mind, high colour, and strong character. Not such character, perhaps, as those who aim at the welfare of the human race would desire to increase, and multiply; but such as many positive moralists prefer to what they call " the washed out type of persons, without any will of their own." In a word, here was the red-faced man.

The style of courteous bluffness, and of pleasant arrogance, which liked him well, and made clever women hate him so, was not at all the cue to suit him now. For now he had to deal, with a man that knew him, and felt for him even less respect, than he still was able to nourish for himself. On this account, George Gaston allowed himself to look as nearly as possible the animal he was—an ill-bred, ill-conditioned man ; who had chosen the evil, rather than the good; and despised the good, because he never could regain it.

Guy Wenlow, the murderer of two women— if verdicts could be trusted—and now the outcast of the moor, was forcing his overhung, and tangled way, to the place of appointment, with such a reckless noise; partly through ferocity, and partly of set purpose. For he wanted to show that he was not afraid of any one, but could roam where he pleased, like a gentleman at large.

Generally, when two big villains meet, for concoction of further villainy, one of them takes the upper hand, and keeps it, in virtue—if the word may so be used—of more skilful, and masterful villainy. This was what Gaston intended to do; and Wenlow was equally resolved to do it. But a man who has dwelt in the desert for a twelvemonth, and mainly been dealing with the larger forms of nature, lies at a sad disadvantage before his fellow, who has never missed a day, in the factory, and mart of lies.

George Gaston smiled at his former comrade, as he broke from the covert into the rugged opening, with his gun at full-cock, and eyes flashing defiance. "Did you think that I would harm you?" he asked rather sadly; "is there no confidence, among old friends?"

"Talk no rubbish," the old friend replied; "if you could gain sixpence by hanging me, and keep your own body out of it, you would do it. What do you want with me? My time is short."

"Your time will be shorter, if you so misuse

it. You are soured by retirement, instead of growing mellow. I am disappointed, by your want of cordiality."

The man of the sheepskins turned away with an oath, and threw his gun on his shoulder. "I came a long way to oblige you," he said; "Good-bye! You will swing before I do."

"Civilization has no sweets for him. There was a time, when he loved potted char. But now he cares only for Dartmoor mutton."

"Gaston," cried the other, coming back with dignity, and yet with some signs of desire about his mouth, "is it potted char? What a memory you have! If you only knew, how sick I am of mutton!"

"It is potted char, from the only house possessing any connection with the genuine fish. The brand is on the top, and the bottom, and the sides, and especially over the place to put the knife in; because of the sad increase of commercial roguery. The smell alone will indicate how genuine it is. A 3 lb. pot, for old lang syne. But alas, there is no true friendship left!"

"How many pots of it have you brought? This is truly kind, on your part, George. No one has shown a bit of care about my likings, ever since every one turned against me. But

what is it you want of me, in return for all this
bribery ? "

" Only a little thing, Guy Wenlow; a trifle
altogether, for a man of your position. I am
half ashamed to give you such a trumpery com-
mission. But it may lead to better things for
both of us, hereafter."

" No mealy mouth about it, George. I care
very little what I do now."

" Well, this is a thing that you will like to
do. You hate any fellow, that sticks up to be
a wonder ? "

" That I do, with all my heart. It is humbug, rank humbug. We are all alike. You
know it, as well as I do."

" Never mind moralizing now. Do you remember a tale I told you, that night when the
lightning was so frightful on the heath ? "

" Every word of it," answered the other, with
a laugh; " for it let me into a little secret, that
even George Gaston was afraid of something.
' Let us talk of something good,' you said, ' the
weather is so awful; let us talk of something
good.' Fie, George, fie, to be a coward of a
thunder-cloud ! "

" If you had seen what I have, ay and felt it
too, you would sing another song, Guy Wenlow.

Some men attract it, some repel. Twice have I been struck; and the colour of my face—but never mind now—it never thunders here."

"That shows your ignorance of the moor. You should hear it rattle round the tors, sometimes. But what am I to do for you? And how much for it?"

"All you have to do for me, is to knock down a small boy. And for that you shall have £5 in gold. Unless you like to do it, from good feeling only. For what chance can you get of spending any money?"

"Gaston, you always were a despicable screw. To knock down a boy, costs five shillings, and expenses. For £5, twenty boys should be knocked down; and you are not the man to pay too much. What you want, is a bigger job than that. Out with it!"

"Well, if you want a big name for it, and small crimes do not suit you, Guy, you may call it the robbery of Her Majesty's mail, as represented by a cobbler's boy. The man of whom I told you that fine story, a cock-a-hoop, a high-flyer, a romantic fool of honour—— "

"You called him none of that, George Gaston, when the lightning was around you. He was a marvel of good works then; and to praise him seemed to protect you in your trembles."

"Pest upon that! I was nervous, I confess. Every one has his weak point, I suppose. What he may be, is no concern of yours. All you have to do, is to look after him for me. And if you do it well, you shall have handsome pay. Even in the wilderness, you want money. Without it, you would have been taken long ago. And, to break into farm-houses, is but onions, and bacon. A little healthy business, on the outskirts of the moor, will cure you of bog ague, and put cash in your woolly pockets. Wenlow, I congratulate you, on your brave appearance."

"Any fool can laugh. You are wasting time. I cannot. My day is divided; and I never knew the value of time, till I had to score it by the shadows."

"And to keep on the shadowy side of the score. Impatient man, I will be brief. Have you ever heard of Christowell?"

"Yes, I know all about it. I have got an eye to the parson's house. You may hear of something I do there."

"Try nothing of the kind. It is a very quiet hole, and must be treated quietly. Under the beacon, lives our friend, who made such a fool of himself years back. There he has got

a sort of hut, and garden—a craze, a bit of mad-
ness, suited to his strange propensities. He
was knocked on the head, in some battle, I
believe; and the earth went in upon his brain,
and stayed there. He is cracked about gardening, and the things the worms do. He pounds
away, and labours with his naked arms, as if he
had been born in a brick-field. I saw him
myself, or I could not have believed it. I was
let in, by a man who knows every rat-hole of the
premises. The fellow was a mass of mould, and
grime, when he might have been rolling in
guineas."

"I like a man of that sort. He cannot be a
sneak," Black Wenlow replied, with a look that
meant, 'like you my friend.' "It will take more
than £5, to make me go against him."

"What a sentimental turn that is! Such a
lesson in morality is worth £5. A man is
enabled to charge for his work, according to his
character; £10 will be very handsome, for a man
of yours. You know the man I mean, from my
description. The chaw-bacons call him 'Captain Larks.' I have no time to tell you, how I
am concerned with his affairs; and if I had, it
would do no good. The practical part of the
matter is, that I want to keep him as he is—

retired, industrious, respectable, and wholly in the dark about his family affairs. He has quitted the world, of his own accord; he is as happy as a king; and I wish him to continue so. His return to civilized life would be a plague to me, as well as a misery to himself. I wish him well, with all my heart; for I always liked a magnanimous fool, a boy who sees the world through his own pea-shooter. Perhaps he has never even heard of me; for I have arisen since his day."

"I have no time to hearken to all these items. I have to watch the shadows, as a painter does. Tell me what I have to do; and never mind the reasons."

"All you have to do is, to keep watch upon the man. He must not go from home, without my hearing of it, by a letter through the old rogue at the *Raven*. And another thing, still more important, is that he must not receive any letters. I shall leave Exeter, by the *Quick-silver*, this evening, having discovered all I want to know at present. On Monday, the lawyers of the family will write to him, having at last found him out, through me, after a score of advertisements had failed. That letter will be due to me; and I must have it. It must go through the post, and bear the proper post-marks; but instead of being delivered to Captain Larks, it must be handed over to your humble servant."

" And you wanted me to rob the mail for £5! Many things amaze me in your nature; but one thing astounds me—your quantity of brass."

" Cheek is now the word for it, since your disappearance from polite society. But the name is bigger than the job, Guy Wenlow. To-morrow will be the first of May. On Wednesday morning, the letter will come to Christowell, about ten o'clock as usual, and be left at the house of James Trickey, the cobbler. A new postage 'envelope,' some new-fangled crotchet for cheap letters, is to be issued on the first of May; with the postage paid, or some such stuff. All Christowell will be goggle-eyed, for a long time after these come to hand. I shall send two dozen dummies to people, whose names I have picked up. Trickey will be mazed, as they call it about here, and attribute all these wonders to the Pixies, and the witches. He won't venture out of sight of his own door, that day; especially at such a time of year, when the evil spirits do their worst. His little boy Bob, who is too young to be afraid, will be

sent up the hill with the captain's letter. Scare
him to the point of death; but don't hurt him."

"You need not tell me that; I am benevolence itself. Very well, I take his letter; and
what then? On the moor are no post-offices."

"But the man at the *Raven* can be trusted.
He makes a good thing out of you. For any
pretty bit of skill, a noble door is opened by all
this new nonsense about cheap letters, and
paying for their carriage beforehand. When
there was eightpence to pay, it could be shown
whether anybody paid the eightpence; but who
will know now, what becomes of a letter, when
the interest of the post-office is to take the dirty
penny, and have no more bother with it? Such
a plan may last a month perhaps; and throughout that month, will be a muddle. All that I
have foreseen; and timed your little plan accord-
ingly. A hideous thing, called an ' envelope '
—because there is no English name for it—will
contain this letter for Captain Larks. All you
have to do, is to take it from the boy, go to the
Raven the same night with it, before any fuss
arises, find my instructions, and follow them."

"That is all very simple, and a credit to you,
Gaston. But excuse my anxiety about the cash.
The sum is a small one; but the times are bad

with me.   These miserly clod-hoppers smuggle off their money to a bank, instead of their bolster, or the thatch.   For a month, I have not known where to turn, for a hit of honest plunder. Even the *Raven* begins to look askew at me."

" That shall be righted; and you must not be too active now, except upon my business.   You have your head-quarters, the Lord knows where, in the depth of this horrible wilderness.   The man of the *Raven* is a very decent fellow, and would sell his good old wife, for a fair con- sideration.   The moor is delightful, at this time of year, and the air ecstatically bracing.   Stock yourself well, to the extent of a sovereign (which I will leave with mine host on account), spend a few days healthfully, in the boggiest quarters of your beat, enjoy my potted char, and some very choice pig-tail, which I will leave for you—a perfect charm for all aches, and agues—and then, on Wednesday morning, earn your balance, repair to the trysting-place, and get it."

" You go on so fast, when you want to slur a point.   Slow and sure, is my style of business. Am I to look for you, at that filthy hole, on Wednesday ? "

" Is there no meaning in the English language ?   I said that you then would find my instructions, and according to them, send back the letter. After that, your care of Captain Larks begins. Lest haply he should hear of things, from any other quarter, which it is his hearty desire, and truest interest, not to know. Having hit upon a clue to him, some half year ago, I have employed some nicety in placing all advertisements, or at least in suggesting the quarter for them, so that none of them should hit him. But now I make a clean breast to the men of law, who have a perfectly just faith in me. By vast exertions, I have found the man. They will write to him, after much sage counsel, a letter for which they will charge two guineas, though it is to go two hundred miles, for one penny. For another penny, it comes back to them. Wonderful is the insolence of this age. How happy are you, who live out of it! Steam-coaches are beginning to run madly all about. Next year they are to come to Bristol. They are taking everybody's land, without his leave. That has something to do with the urgency of this matter. It outrages all one's sense of justice. But, thank heaven, there are still some people, who know what is right, and stick to it!"

"And foremost of them all, George Gaston.

Very well, I know now what you want, and will carry it out most faithfully. Where will the tobacco be ? I want that first. If you knew what stuff I am obliged to smoke—— "

" You shall have it to-night, with your outfit, at the *Raven*. Lay aside, once and for all, your most narrow idea, that I stint anything. Of all men, I am the most liberal, when it pays."

" To me, you should be more than liberal, George. Whose doing is it, that I lead this life ? Who first led me, to despise my home, to want to be more than I was meant for, to gamble away my poor father's savings, to rob my sister, to break my mother's heart—— "

" Guy Wenlow, this tenderness is not thrown away on me. It proves that your heart is in the right place still ; though it may have sadly roamed away from it. But we must not linger. The whole world is in a hurry. Nobody looks back ; everybody forward. Repentance, and remorse, are a pair of old samplers. The *Quick-silver* average is fourteen miles an hour ; and the horses must be changed, in thirty seconds, to show that they can beat steam-coaches. When you were a sporting character, Guy Wenlow, with £50 on each side of your stomach, how you would have loved to sit behind those horses! But they summon me; I seem to hear them neigh."

The better of the two men turned away, to hide the tear which the memory of his mother, or perhaps of the horses, had called forth. Then he swung his heavy gun, upon his shoulder, and made off. "One little trifle I forgot to mention," the other shouted after him, " a thing that will make you stick the closer to your duty. The captain's daughter is the loveliest girl, that can be found, even in Devonshire. You are an admirer of the sex. *Verbum sat.*"

" We are told, that the devil lives on Dartmoor," cried the outcast; " but now he means to come to and fro, by the *Quicksilver.*"

" Go thy way. The fool, and the woman, have privilege of last word," Gaston muttered. Then putting away a pistol, which had been hidden near his fingers, he discharged into his mouth a more peaceful implement, known among travellers by the same name. With his high colour heightened, he arose, and left the dell; whose beauty was not impaired by his departure.

CHAPTER XV.

THE DANCING TREE.

AMONG the few places that now keep shops, on
the threadbare skirt of Dartmoor, one of the
kindest, and most tranquil-minded, is that little
town, Moreton Hampstead.

A man of fine leisure, and liberal ease, with a
ripe turn for contemplation, may be looked for
—if any one is rude enough to want him—first
near the tap of his favourite inn ; then about the
reading-room, or post-office ; after that, clearly
at the farrier's shop; and for the rest of the
day, on the bridge, with a pipe in his mouth,
and hands in pocket.

The great defect of Moreton is therefore this,
that it owns no bridge of any kind, for such
transcendent uses.   But in plea of that, it may
well be urged (if any man there can be urgent)
first that if any bridge were needed, no one
could ever find the energy to build it ; and next

that no genuine Moreton man would go forth to a bridge, for his lounge, while he can get it, right happily, on his own window-ledge. If ever he is wanted, which very seldom happens, there he may be found, during those short periods, when he is not feeding, or profoundly asleep. Now as to those two *alibis*, the former is strictly sacred. The shop-door is bolted, and the bell unhung; and from twelve o'clock, till two, the only business considered, is the commerce of the interior. Then if anybody, scanty of good manners, thumps upon the door, why just let him thump again. With a relish, as of pickles, or of very cool cucumber, the hearty tradesman smacks his lips, and labours at the self-help most congenial to him,—a large help of very lofty order of mutton. If, at two o'clock, he unbolts his door, and rehangs his bell, he may be taken at the moment, and goaded into a shout to his wife, to know the price of something, now hanging in his window. However, if his wife makes no reply—as generally happens, for she is of his own race—he will ask the brisk customer, how much he has been in the habit of giving for the article. If the customer forgets, or prefers not to tell, because he expects to get it cheaper here, the worthy shopkeeper

talks about invoices, which he cannot lay his
hand upon just now, but will do so at his
earliest leisure, and the gentleman may take it,
and come, and know the price to-morrow. Then
he retires for his afternoon nap, having done a
striking stroke of business.

Nevertheless, there are two people often wide-
awake at Moreton. One is the boy, with two
buckets, and a mop, who invades the gentle
streets, soon after breakfast, and stirs the narrow
echoes with his constant cry—" Wash yer win-
ders for 'ee!"   As nobody ever washes his own
windows, and the wind asserts its hereditary,
and perhaps etymologic, right to invest every
window with a coat of granite grime, this boy
has got to move both arms at once, and becomes
a pleasant sight, for those who never do so.

Or rather, those who do so, only when they
are a-dancing. Because of so being asleep all
day, and having no bridge to yawn upon,
Moreton is—or was, until a railway rushed into
the bottom—" the chiefest place for dancing, to
be found in merry Devonsheer." While a man
slumbers sweetly, against the partition, that
severs his nice little parlour from his shop (it
is needless to say, upon which side he is) another
man, knowing the trick of the door, runs in

(though nothing else could ever make him run) and handling him by the head, against the wall, pulsatively, stirs up the muffled drum of his outer ear, by blowing down the conch of his other palm into it—"Ball to-night! Zax o'clock." "How much be tickutts?" asks the firm reposer, with a rub of his eyes, and a tingle in his head. "Zaxpince aich—dree vor a zhillun." Then he feels in the fork of his clothes, and pays a shilling.

This is the other man, who keeps on moving, and whips round the corners, quicker than a window can go up. He gets up the dances, and he knows the way to do it, calling on the ladies first, and putting clearly to them, that all the gentlemen in the place are wild, about getting them to come, but on no account would trouble them to come, except just as they are. Nothing in the way of dress could make them look better than they do now; and he chins up his fiddle, and touches two strings. Every lady looks demure, and says that she really dislikes dancing, and did hope to have heard the last of it. But rather than disappoint her neighbours, she will take one ticket. Then he twangs again; and with an eye to strict economy, she takes six.

Behold, how unjust a thing it is to attempt to be too accurate! There is another active man in Moreton Hampstead, and his name is Timothy Pugsley. Happily for the town, which never could endure three moving spirits, the greater part of his time goes away, among the lanes, and across the hills. When he comes home at night, with Teddy, the two of them want stable. They are stiff about their joints, and say to themselves, and to one another, that they would go ten miles more, if needful, but can see no more to do to-day, except victuals; and are glad of it. Teddy has a mash, with hay to follow, and oats enough to dream of; and Timothy has a pan of fried potatoes, browning on the fire, with a plate turned over them, and bacon making little pops around the plate's edges, and jumping up at every pop, in a hurry to be tasted.

Timothy feels, as well as smells, after twelve hours on the moor, this joy; and he thanks the Lord, to find a warm house round him, a safe deliverance from robbers, storm, and accident, an uncommonly sharp appetite, with victuals fit to sharpen it, and a wife, who keeps his house in order, and can fry potatoes.

Yet, the most lively, and dissipated being, in all the town of Moreton, is neither the window-washing boy, nor the great Chorægus, nor even Timothy Pugsley; but a tree, of great weight, and very prominent position, and old enough to know better. Whether its lineage is from one that danced to the lyre of Orpheus, or whether any Dryad with a tripping foot possesses it,—at any rate, this is the dancing tree. For many years now, it has left off dancing, even if it ever did begin, and has to be contented with the legal truth—" who does through another, does the thing himself." And to make sure, it does it, through a great many others.

Especially, on the first of May, when the festival of Pales—as the learned tell us—is well observed by Christians. Instead of putting up a May-pole then, and frolicking around it, in a Pixy ring, the young folk of Moreton have their frisks among the verdure, without dread of dewy feet, or toes stuck in a mole-hill. High up in the tree, which stands in an elbow of scraggy street, they hoist, and fix a timber platform, strong enough to bear the vehemence of feet, not too aerial. The boughs of the patulous tree, above the bole, afford a noble amplitude; and a double ring of hay-rope, roven fast around the branches, provides the most headlong couple with a chance of preserving their necks, when valuable.

"Missy, you'm looking crule weist, and peaky," said Master Pugsley to Miss Arthur, when he was come with another load of pots, towards the end of April; " rackon, that Dicky Touchwood be a' plaguing on 'e. I knows what it be, my own sen, Missy; my good Missus, forgive me for the zame! Never could I zee a purty wench, when I were young, wi'out longing to make up to her. Excoose of me, Missy, if too free of spache. I only tarks what cooineth natteral. To my rank of laife, and conzeiderin' the difference. And you knows it too, by the colour on your chakes."

" Mr. Pugsley, you should mind your own business. Your business is to deliver 144 pots, without any cracks in them."

" Bless 'e, Miss Rose, and I have doed it. They little sniggers is what cometh in the baking. Never yet sot I down a deliverance more claner. But you was a very little one, when first I knowed you, and growing bigger every spare-time, wi'out conzeiderin' of it. Why you used to make nort of kissing me, and never ax wuther no pots was cracked! But the chillers grow'th up, Miss, by will of the Lord, and doeth, like their veythers, and their moothers doed avore them. And it coom across my maind, Miss, by rason of the dancing-time, that you was to be warneded of being a young 'ooman now, and no moother to look arter 'e. My waife zaith to me, afore prim taime of slumbering— 'no moother, Tim, to look arter her; and the cappen no better than a hanvil-smiter; her wanteth a light hand; Tim, you do it.' Zum- taimes, my waife gooeth wrong about men's business, or consarning of me, or even of my datters, when they don't desarve it; but never in her judgment of the gentry, Miss."

"I am very much obliged, I am sure, to any- body, who wishes to be kind to me, and fancies that I want it. But none of you seem to under- stand, that I have nothing to complain of. I have heard enough, of what ladies do, from a young lady, who is here, staying in our house; and if nobody wanted pity more than I do, the world would be very happy, Mr. Pugsley."

"Zo 'un be," replied the carrier stoutly. "I zung a zong, all the way from Marton, 's marn- ing; and a' can zing a zong, wi' ony of the gallery. But I likes to see the young volk a dancing too. The Lard hath made it natteral to 'un. And when I zeed your little voot, a' comin' from your pettygoat, I said to myzell,

what a dancer her would make! Do 'e come,
and zee our May-dancing, that's a dearie."

"I dare say, your May-dance is very pretty,
or at any rate very queer," said Rose; "but it
is not a fit place for ladies, I'm afraid. How
can you keep rough people out?"

"If any man offendeth, in zider, ale, or
langowich," the carrier answered austerely; "us
kicketh 'un out o' the tree, wi'out no rasoning,
and a' cometh down zober, on the backside of his
head. Never has no call to do it twice, Miss.
'Twud do 'e good to zee 'un; and our upstair
windy looketh down into the thick of it, like a
bird's nestie. Wull 'e coom, if Cappen be agray-
able thereto?"

Rose laughed at the idea that her father
would consent, and cheerfully promised to go, if
he should do so. Then Master Pugsley, in a
bold yet crafty manner, made approaches to the
captain; and if truth ever did admit ductile, or
elastic, fibre into the close grain of her heart, the
carrier found out how to make her, "wi'out
telling no lies"—as he himself acknowledged.

In this way it was settled then, that Mistress
Pugsley (who could drive, as well as her husband—and her husband as well, according to
some folk, whose business it was none of) should

come in the Sunday-shay, at one o'clock on Monday, and put up the horse (who was to be borrowed, from a man who owed a bill of two years' standing) and dine in the kitchen, with Moggy the maid; though the captain said no; but Tim Pugsley was firm, that his wife should not sit to a red-legged table, and the life he would lead with her afterwards. " Her could do up all the chany, and the zilver, like a looking-glass;" he said, for fear of having seemed to go against her dignity.

Then, about three o'clock, they were to start, in the Sunday-shay borrowed from the White Hart Inn; and so (inasmuch as it would be absurd to spare a horse belonging to a man who owed him money) they might get to Moreton very well, by half-past four, and show Miss the shops, and the Punch and Judy, and wise pig, come from Exeter.

Nothing can ever hope to be done now, according to its calculation; because of the many other things, all equally busy, that come in the way of it. But forty years ago, the rush was scarcely half-begun yet; and there still was time to live in. Mrs. Pugsley came, with the light shay, and the pony, who could properly afford to be thrashed, because his master could not pay.

And Rose, although her mind might be considered rather large, was unable to help getting into high spirits, at the little change, and bit of fun, in front of her. But another, and a far more important person, was grieved, and sore wounded at heart, by such an outbreak.

"Then, am I to be left to myself all the day, while you go to see the chaw-bacons capering?" Dicky Touchwood asked, when he heard of what was toward; and his voice was rich with a melancholy sound.

"You must not be left alone, because you are never any company to yourself," his fair attendant answered, in the kindest manner; "but that has been provided for, before this was thought of. Miss Perperaps has promised to come up, and sit with you, and read you a story-book, until you go to sleep. And I am to be home again, by one o'clock to-morrow; you will scarcely even know, that I have been away at all. And perhaps, I shall be able to make you laugh. I never saw anybody laugh like you. I am only afraid that it is bad for you."

"Do I laugh? Then I am sure I never mean it. It is all Spotty's fault; because she never cares for anything. I don't like young ladies of that character at all."

"You must never say that. It sounds un-grateful. If Miss Perperaps had been your own sister, she could not have done more for you."

"That makes it all the worse, and drives me wild. Why should people I don't care for, do me all the good that gets done for me; and the really nice ones take no notice? And they never seem to know, how it urges me!"

"Mr. Touchwood, it seems to me that you should rather ask, why you don't care for the people that are kind to you, and do you all the good, that would not get done for you, unless you had them to do it."

"Very well. I dare say you think me un-grateful. But I am put out, because I shall not see you, very likely for two whole days. And the only pleasure I get now, is to look at you, Miss Arthur."

"Good-bye. Your dear mamma will be here at three o'clock; and I hope that she will say you are a great deal better. It is most unlucky, that whenever she comes, you should happen to fall back so, and be so languid, and low-spirited. It makes Lady Touchwood disbelieve the doctor; and she goes away, with such a sigh. Even if you feel worse than usual, you should try to put a cheerful face on; and especially to-day, when your sister is coming, for the first time, to see you. I am sure that you can walk very nicely, if you try."

"You never seem to enter into my case at all," Dicky Touchwood complained, as she passed out of hearing; "I don't want to go away. I like the place; I like the captain; I like the apple-fritters; and somebody even better still. In fact, I like everything, except the medicines. And if they would only allow me the right thing in malt, I'll be blest, if I'd ever get well again."

But his lovely young hostess, with all her good nature, was getting rather tired of his vapours, and vagaries. Her main delight was to be with her father, to help him, and hand him his needs, and be ready with a smile (when that was one of them) and be able, at supper-time, to tell him how much he had done, if he dared to reproach himself. But ever since this boy tumbled in among them, instead of looking after her vines and roses, she must give up her time to be looked at by him. And this made her glad, to get away to Moreton.

Timothy Pugsley's "little ouze"—as he called his most highly respectable dwelling—was as full of deep corners, and heavy over-hangings, and loopings, and humpings, and jags, and juttings, as the loftiest artist could desire to find, on a tour, or upon a friend's property. We take, at the present moment, deep interest in our forefathers; because they were so ignorant, in comparison with ourselves; and we doubt their *differentia*—as it used to be called, and used to be settled, before all wisdom went to flux. But if anything can be inferred about them (where all is inference, deference none), it seems to be, that they were fond of corners. They loved a deep corner; as we love a flat, whether vertical, or horizontal; and they liked to see shadow, as much as we hate it.

The carrier's house went up and down, and in and out, almost as freely as his cart did on the roads; and the roof carried fodder enough for a horse, as Teddy observed, with a watering mouth. No climbers were wanted, to cluster the windows, for the droopers clothed them amply—creeping Jenny, and run-away Jack, and the many forms of house-leek, with golden moss to brighten them. No rakes came near them, neither besom of destruction; their only enemy was the wind; and that they passed on into the chimney-pots.

"Now, if you plaize, Miss, this cornder hath

been claned for 'e," said Master Pugsley to Miss Arthur, after a magnificent tea downstairs. "'Tis the very best place in all Marton town, for spyin' of they ranties. And wi'out you putts your head var vorth, ne'er a wan of 'em can see 'e. Viddles be toonin' up, a'ready. Many is the time, I've a' doed it, with the best of 'em. Zuntimes I wush I wor a lad again, and no vam'ly. Don't 'e tell that to my Missus, though."

"I've aheered 'e," said Mrs. Pugsley, panting up the creaky stairs, for she was fat exceedingly; "I've aheered 'e, Tim; and I be 'sheamed of 'e. Lor, Miss Rose, when my Timmy wor a buy, you could have put your two hands round him, what with his chronicles, and his asterisks! Nobody said a' wud ever grow up; but a' did; and a' wanteth to do so again, wi'out no waife to do's vittles for 'un."

"You've dooed your own too," said the carrier with a smile. "How well her look'th, Miss Rosie, and chakes so bright as you'rn a'most!"

"By rason I gotten a good man to keep me. Now Missy, shall I stop with you, and tell 'e who the vork be; or wad 'e zoonder baide aloun? Tim must be off, adoin' of a zaight of things. Nort can be done in this here town, wi'out Tim Pugsley."

"Oh, please to stop with me," said Rose; "I should never know anything about it—and indeed I would not stop, to shut you out from your own window. And Sally, and Milly, and Billy, must come. Why, what are they going to do already? The sunset is on the church-tower still, and the moon is as pale as an oyster-shell; but.they mean to begin—I declare they do!"

They meant to begin, and more than that, they did begin without delay, and with strong intention to go on. For the girls there was a tallat ladder, to be mounted, according to their manifold natures; some making a great fuss (for fear of falling, without being noticed), some skipping up shyly, before any one could think of them, some ascending slowly, with a gaze of large unconsciousness; and others smiling, with their skirts tucked in, to prove what management can do. The lads, upon the other hand, had too much of their own to do, to be over-nice in criticism. Their only way up to the dancing-stage, was a half-inch rope, hanging down from a bough, and anointed well with mutton-suet. Also, at the landing place, where an active lad might stick his heels in, invidious fellows, who had climbed already, and wished to keep the platform to themselves, showed a narrow-minded tendency to push away any better-looking lad, who was aspiring to the girls. And a combat ensued, which was pleasant to behold.

"They've been, and gotten our best stable lantern!" Mrs. Pugsley cried indignantly. "Fie upon Tim, they get over him so! One of them scrapers scrapeth with a book. Some saith 'tis larnin', and some saith 'tis hignorance. Girt hignorance, to my mind, vor to viddle wi' a copy-book. There they gooth—fust couple right, and turn once! Zim'th no more nor yesterday, as I wur doin' of it. Vaive and thirty years agone, miss; and us used to cry 'Boney' for the gals to shake to; and if you said it now, they would stare, and ax the manin'."

"But they seem to shake very well, without it, Mrs. Pugsley. How wonderfully they go in and out! I never saw anything half so pretty. And how beautifully they keep time; though they seem to be laughing, instead of being serious! I have seen a ball of very high society at Exeter, just that I might know how to understand it, through the cracks of the door, and from the cock-loft; but it frightened me sadly to look at them; because they seemed to dance one step, and frown two."

"The karlity knows what is best for 'em, miss"—Mrs. Pugsley had been cook in a very good family, and never meant to sink the difference,—"but our lads, and wenches, if soever they comes crossways, with royal authority, and the viddles going twang, and the moon a' shaining bright, and a man like Tim, and a 'ooman like me, looking on agin' all unpropriety, they sayeth to themselves, and to wan anither—'us may carry on now, and spake the word that cometh upward.' And then they goo'th on, for more nor thiccy."

"Whatever they are thinking of, they look very nice, and they do it very well, and their manners are so good! Why, they bow to one another continually!"

"Not they, miss; never a one of them. 'Tis the branches makes them duck their heads, for fear of an orkard clout on 'em. Good manners coom'th convanient so."

Whatever their manners were, they enjoyed them, and with nature's help looked well. For the large moon began to come loftily into the middle of their doings, and to make them clear. The maidens were the first to feel her influence, and look at her, and hold their heads up well, and have deep imaginations. Then the youths took the temper of the moment from them, and found a higher beauty of the distance in their eyes, and upon their lips a graver, and a sweeter, turn of smiling.

Even the fiddlers three, and the piper, worthy to perform before King Cole, took a softer stroke of melody, and worked their funny-bones more gently. Perched up in the branches, with a rope to keep them to it, and a tankard refilled at the end of every tune, they set their heels firmer, and bedewed their hands, and nodding to one another, glided sweetly, into a plaintive and wistful air, with their pots shining chastely, in the light across the churchyard. To the movement of their music, lads and lasses circled slowly, well content with measure more sedate, and time for serious steps.

For the moonlight wavered in the play of their vibration, and put a selvage to their shadows (where the lamp shone in), and followed in and out of pale innumerable buds, and rested upon nothing, but the rugged lines of heart-wood, scarred with the jocosities of by-gone dancers ; whose names were wearing out, upon the tombstones down below.

"Now, Missus Littlejan, you can't get out of it no more," Rose heard Carrier Pugsley say to a very pretty woman, who was standing in a doorway. "You was the sproylest of the lot, dree years running, and not a maid among 'em can put a foot out wi' 'e, now times. You be burnin' to be at it, and your chakes con‑ fesseth. They be arl gooin' on, crule weist, and heavy like. I dunno, what hath come across the lads, since I wor one of 'em. Call your good man, that's a dear, and goo up the skip to aupway."

"And I can goo up, as suent as ever," the young matron answered, with a longing glance; " in the looment of the laight, they do zim weist. But conzeider the babby, Maister Pugsley, con‑ zeider of my husband's babby."

"Drat the babby; or bless 'un, I shud zay. Our Zally will tend 'un. Zally coom peart, and vang Mrs. Littlejan's babby."

Then Rose saw the brisk little woman go up, and heard a loud hail to her, the Queen of former May times; and a merry tune broke forth, and the mood was all quick stroke again. Then Pugsley, rejoicing to see a bright success, went up the ladder to the dance himself; for he could tread a measure still, with heels, in

lieu of toeing it. But Sally, who would have
to give account of his doings to her mother,
fastened upon him the whole speculation of her
blue eyes, and left the infant Littlejohn to the
ministry of angels.

"Do you see that wild horse up the hill?"
cried Rose; "he is tossing, and straining, and
dashing at his reins; I expect to see him break
loose every moment."

"Lor, miss, no! Never trouble about he,"
Mrs. Pugsley answered calmly. "'Tis only
baker Pollard's young gray nag; he hooketh
him up there, twaice a day. And he riglar
furmiteth about, like that."

"What is there to stop him, if he breaks
loose with the cart? And here come those
Punch and Judy people, close behind him! Oh,
he is loose, he is off!"

Without another word, she too was off, down
the crooked staircase, like a rabbit through a
hole, and out at the front door, which luckily
was open. The baby of the Littlejohns was in
the street before her, making just a little crawl,
and trying to say "boo," with the mad horse
striking fire, in his dash down hill upon it, and
the wheels behind him flying, like a kettle at a
dog's tail. Away ran a score of louts snigger-

ing, and yelling; and women justly screamed; for death was dashing on the baby.

With a set heart, and firm bound of all the life within her, Rose Arthur stood in the very middle of the narrow roadway, before the poor baby, and pulled her white hat off, and threw it at the forehead of the horse, almost upon her. Swerving with a wild plunge—for check himself he could not—he flung the cart high in the air, and flew on, with the reins, like a lasso, whirling after him. The loop caught the leg of baby Littlejohn; but Rose threw it up; and the tire of the jumping wheel tore off a lock of her long scattered hair. With a dash, and a clash, all the peril was gone by, and the roar, and the scream, echoed further down the street.

Rose Arthur lay stunned by the whirr of the wheel, within a single inch of her lovely little ear; if the wheel had not leaped, at the plunge of the horse, it must have gone over her slim white neck. When she came to herself, she was in the strong arms of a young man, who had rushed forth to save her, but too late to do more than pick her up, and worship her.

"She is killed, I do believe, you disgraceful pack of cowards!" he cried to the fellows, who came crowding now around. "I never saw anything so grand, and so barbarous. Go, and fetch your mothers; it is all that you are fit for." There were plenty of brave young men around; but their presence of mind had failed them.

"Thank you; I don't think that I have been hurt," said the maiden in a whisper, and looking shyly up at him; "only stupidly frightened. But how is the baby?"

"The baby is laughing in the arms of its mother. But you, who are worth ten thousand babies——"

"Please to put me down, sir. I am not so giddy now. Oh, here comes Mrs. Pugsley! I am most thankful to you, though I cannot tell you properly."

"You be off, young man!" cried the carrier's wife, for the Westcombes were unknown on this side of the moor; "you han't done no harm, and you han't done no good. Be off, I tell 'e. Bain't no place for you. Hus be going to examine this young leddy." The dismissal was urgent; there was no plea for lingering. Everybody seemed to say, "What do you want here? Who are you, to abuse the Moreton folk?" With a deep bow, meant for Rose, but received by Mrs. Pugsley, in the ample region where she tied her apron strings, he accepted the decision of the public, and was off.

But all excellent intentions must have some luck somewhere; if capable of paying for it, and eager so to do. And Pollard, the baker, who was sitting on his flour-bin, sadly scoring, with his white material, a loss of more than £3 10s., from the breakage of shaft, and bolt, and panel, and a spring of five leaves, and the gray colt's knee, and a host of little items of the ruefullest arithmetic—he did signal justice to that young man's lofty character, without assigning reason.

But Mrs. Pollard knew the reason; and she kept it close as dough, until the brewer's charm begins. The reason was, that young Jack Westcombe, before he started for his long night-walk, provided a curl paper for a curl. Or, to put it more precisely, he gave a £5 note for the silky tress, which he had discovered between the sprung tire, and cracked felloe, of the cart's surviving wheel. He might have had it gladly for five shillings; but love scorned such an insult.

CHAPTER XVI.

"THE RAVEN."

Much has been said well, and written even
better, about the vast progress of the age, in all
things, except honesty, courage, and kindliness.
These are of small account; when a man runs,
his loose ends must blow out behind him.

Everybody said, in Christowell, where the
people have always been considered very wise,
that the Government of the United Kingdom
was conspiring to rob honest people. When a
man got a letter, his first business used to be, to
pay for it, and then to stick it on his mantel, for
a picture; until such time, as a great book-scholar
should be in need of twopence, for a glass of
beer. But whoso got a letter for a penny, or a
thank'e, was it fair to expect him to pay twopence, every time he got it read to him? The
opinion of Christowell, headed by the landlord
(into whose till, every twopence must have

travelled), was distinctly, and deliberately, this —that the post had no right to deliver letters for a penny, without providing somebody, to come and read them *gratis*.

This matter had scarcely been under discussion, so much as four months, when a new upset arose. The cobbler, in every village good enough to have one, was regarded by the Government, in all the new arrangements, as the first claimant to the postmastership, in right of his professional complicity with wax. Hence it will be manifest, that Mr. James Trickey, though curt perhaps of graceful courtesy, was strictly correct from an official point of view, in his highly suggestive demonstration to Carrier Pugsley, when rooted in the rut. No man should ever be condemned, at first sight, whatever part of his organization is foremost to woo stern criticism.

The mind of that postmaster was in a state of unusual tension, and wholly indifferent, as the mind in office must be, to any good works beyond its own vocation. His appointment was new, and he had to justify it; for the village, having done without a post-office for centuries, not only saw no need of it, but had a right to be indignant; though the elder folk, having larger toleration, said, " Let un coom ; her taime wun't be long. 'Tis a get up to sell gate-postesses ; and nubbody buyeth they, in these here parts."

Master Trickey knew better, and was proud to do so ; and holding himself above inquiries, would neither take, nor make them. In refusing to answer, he was right, as a man always is, when he knows nothing ; but in sternly resolving not to ask, he showed perhaps less wisdom. For although he could read with some fluency in the Bible, and do the fourteen generations, he could not make out the tremendous words, in which the vast era of progress began. He was told, in his orders, to " communicate, in anticipation of emergency, with the central administration." This puzzled him, for it sounded like the Prayer-book, only bigger.

Now if he had taken this question to his minister (as exhorted to do, in a book, whose clear English shall never be surpassed by the very biggest writer), his difficulties might have been duly solved, and he must have got an order for a pair of fishing-boots ; which by reason of his " reticence," was quite lost to the parish, and even went as far away as Newton Abbot. For Mr. Short made a point of knowing, what his own folk were up to, and a point of honour when his letters were concerned; and he never made surer of anything in his life, than that such a wiseacre as Jem Trickey would be at his door, thrice every day, with something to be explained three times. There scarcely could be a more liberal man than the parson, a strict Conservative—a race of men who practise true, and let the others prabble truculent philosophy. And now the parson proved all this; for he paid 5*s. extra*, rather than wear a pair of boots, to the profit of such a Radical.

Master Trickey felt these things, and lamented in the bosom of his family. In public however, he declared, that such considerations were beneath him, that an officer of the Crown must be above small byses, either of leather or of learning; and parson's behaviour should have no effect upon him, no more than to keep one pew buttoned on a Sunday, and the letters for the vicarage to the tail of the delivery. But even before his grievance ripened, or the vicar knew that it was growing, this haughty layman bit the dust, at the feet of Mother Church, and Father Short.

For a very remarkable thing happened now,

one of those facts which defy defiant reason,
and set at nought all purest process of induc-
tion, deduction, or *reductio ad absurdum*. Christowell remembered many things, that could not be
explained; but these had left off happening
lately, so that the upstarts grew too bold, and
the veterans (rasped of the crust of reason, by
the roughness of hard life) told one another
that the Lord was now clock-time, to read they
young cockahoops a warning. And a warning
now was read to them, which made them shake
in their moonlit beds, and turned all argument
into agreement, and stupid young fancy into
stubborn faith again. For the author of evil,
who never can be satisfied even with his own
exertions, and is famed for " looking over Darty-
more," as keenly as over his own pet Lincoln,
in this crisis of " postal development," came
officially, as the great father of lies, to look
after letters, and robbed the mail.

Jem Trickey had a son whose name was Bob,
a truthful boy (comparatively speaking) and
one who could be trusted largely, if he were
not tempted. Neither was that the only thing
remarkable about him; for he was also a boy
that kept his pockets buttoned, and his heels
together. He had tight little calves, like smart

balls of blue worsted, and forks of Nankin—
called in high society " breeches "—which ran
up to his middle, when his legs began to run.
And his legs ran often; for he was a very
earnest boy, eager to be the very foremost of
his age, an example to the other boys—the
which they pelted stones at—to the girls a
riddle, and in larger view intended for a post-
man of letters at a penny.

This boy was fortunate in the possession of a
parent, who not only had keen perception of his
genius, but also the power to make it pay.
Under the new Act of Parliament, Bob, being
early of age at fourteen, was appointed to the
salary of head-postman, and his father cut him
out a pair of cowskin gaiters. No other postal
district could compare with this, for innocence,
and charity, and the absence of ill-will; because
the population was so scanty. Yet even here,
there were people found to say, that sometimes
it was possible to have too much leather.

Now the weather was fine, and the time of
year beginning to be cheerful, and abundant, with
variety of flowers. Every man, leaning on his
shovel in a meadow (which is one of the things
that he is most inclined to do) was pleased, and
yet saddened to behold the same things coming

up, that used to come up a great many years
ago, when he was a child, and spent hours with
them. Ah, the times were better then! He
got his victuals, without labouring, he ran about,
and played, and slept, whenever he was minded;
the taste of everything was better, and the size
much larger, and every year put on his life was
strength, instead of stiffness. But for all that,
if the Lord came now, and said, " Will you go
back again?"—he would think no more of
doing so, than the flowers to shrink back into
bud, and be buried in the root again.

Sam Slowbury did not particularly go through
that, or any other process of mind, as he was
leaning on his shovel; for his nature was not to
think a thought that it could help, any more
than to dream a dream—which he did yearly—
or to do a rapid stroke of work, the which he did
never. But conscience is the guide of duty, as
many learned moralists have shown, and can
show again; and the proof of the pudding is in
the after-taste. Sam Slowbury's conscience only
told him, that he ought to have more wages.
Captain Larks, who could not afford to give
romantic wages, was paying Sam now, one and
tenpence a day, and Sam did the value of tenpence. He was turning up a mixen, in a

meadow near the lane, or rather he was helping it to turn itself; while Mopsy, the cow, with creative pride looked on, and increased in her own self-esteem. Then Slowbury stood more still than ever, if possible, while he stroked the cow; and she, like a very faithful creature, made no other movement than a kinkle in her tail. Everything was pleasant, everything was gracious; there seemed to be a richness of green upon the grass, and a delicate blue in the air, and a desire of the weather to be kind, and happy. Sam felt it; and it added to his leisure, and benevolence, and the way in which he looked about.

"I dun'now as ever I zeed a vainer marnin' coom out o' the top of the sky," he said, with a truth of observation, not often to be found in our most accomplished weather-clerks; for if the fine morning comes from the horizon, the issue of the day is doubtful. "But who be thiccy coming up by graveyard? Jem Cobbler's buy, zure as I be a zinner!" The identity of the boy was the most important question, that had occurred since breakfast-time. Sam even went a yard or two, up the bank, to get a more masterly view of him, and established his shovel in the happiest attitude, for support and comfort.

But so persistent is human care, and so vast the activity of the human mind, that no sooner was it settled beyond dispute, that the figure approaching was the cobbler's son, than another question, even more absorbing, rose defiantly— Whatever could be compelling this scion of leather, to wear out his paternal boots, like that?

For Slowbury could not see, although he used his eyes with diligence, the thing the boy had in his hand, and largely in his head as well. It was one of the new " Mulready envelopes," just come down from London ; and the head of the boy was unsound about it ; because he had never seen the likes before ; and now he had got five-and-twenty of them, mainly for people who could not read. " Deliver fust to they as can intar-pret," his father, who was nearly mazed at the size of the bags, gave orders ; " 'tothers may baide up to next church-time. Goo with Cap-pen's fust ; them as payeth for their boots desarveth fust shoeleather."

Slowbury stood, and watched the progress of this boy with pleasure. But presently he beheld a thing, which made him throw his shovel down, and sit, and bless the angels, who alone can fend the pixies. From the corner of the churchyard, where the tombs lay thickest, a tall figure, flaring in the sun, leaped forth, with a wonderful explosion, and a cloud of pitchy smoke. Sam was ready to swear that he was not mistaken, in seeing nothing more for at least five minutes, and then if it was anything to bear an affidavit, it was the chap from the gravestones jumping, out of the cloud, to the top of the church-tower. And sure enough, when seven unmarried men were sent to the top of the church-tower, they found a place where the moss had been knocked off, and they came down according to their speed, declining (as soon as their breath was restored to them) to go up any more, unless they were strung up to the bell-beams. This proved every syllable, that came from the mouth of Slowbury; out of which came very little (as soon as he knew what he was about) without a great deal of very solid, and highly liquid substance going in, at the sole charge of the inquirer.

There is no justice to be traced, in the affairs of men or boys, without dreadful ingenuity. What had Sam done, to make a pocket out of this affair, more than lean on his shovel, and arouse himself to look a bit, and regard with satisfaction the distance of the miracle? Even when the cloud passed off, and the church was

as bright as she ought to be, this man discovered
that his duty to his master strictly forbade him
to approach what he had witnessed. He re-
treated to another mixen, nearer to the house,
where a man at work might hear the wholesome
cocks a-crowing, and the thumping of the churn
at dairy. And he took Mopsy with him, for
company, because his heart was in the frimitts.

On the other hand, the real hero of this
strange adventure not only sucked no profit
thereout, and no increase of character, but
received knotted strap from his father, and was
threatened of his life, if he told a word of it.
And so do the greatest events get deformed,
(when chance has protected them from smother-
ing), that only two people in Christowell—the
postmaster, and his gaitered son, could find any
motive for that outbreak of the Evil One, except
the sad nature of his constitution.

But the nature of the human creature always
has some spotty places, where the good light
enters. Black Wenlow was glad, that his out-
rush from the tombs, and shower of fireworks
of his own construction, scared the poor boy
so, that no blow was needed; as he fell on his
back and cast away the letter; for feeling is
swifter than thought, and Bob felt that these

wicked inventions brought Satan upon him. Then the sheep-skinned villain vanished, not over the tower, but into a cross cut which led him to the moor.

There is a house, or at any rate was then, far away, among the hills, and hollows, from any other place, where people dwell. How anybody came to dwell there, none but those, who knew the ins and outs of mining on the waste, can pretend to say, if even they can do it. But there this miserable building stood; and a man, who was no more miserable than his fellow-men, had his home there. The savage wilderness, iron-browed hills, and rocks of peaky profile, like a row of hideous giants, were more to the taste of Gruff Howell, than the sweetest landscape, and the kindest sun. To take the rough and the smooth together, is a test of magnanimity; but Howell took the rough, without the smooth, in fare and footing, in climate and in clothes, and in company, whenever he got any to enjoy.

It was said, by the gentler folk afar, that he deserved no better; himself not being fit company for a Christian; and if he had his due, he would be swinging now in chains, as a pirate, on the hill of landscape looking over Plymouth

Sound. But instead of that, he kept the
Raven, by the side of a mine-road long dis-
used ; and no idle rumour disturbed him there ;
for his customers were the moor-men only, a
silent, hard-living, and wandering race. But
even they asked one another, sometimes, about
the queer couple, Griffith Howell, and his wife.

The house had been built by the miners of
old, and therefore was substantial, and well-
squared. For some granite masonry, as fair as
need be wished for—including the tower of
Christowell church, which they built in wholesome gratitude for a great success—has been
done around the moor, and upon it, by the
miners. And they must have been sturdy
fellows, to have reared the *Raven*, without
being blown out of the windows.

For here are strong concourse, and mighty
deliverance, of every wind that sweeps the sea,
buffets the land, or scours the sky. It is a
hollow of the hill-crest well contrived, as the
chimneys of new houses are, to suck down the
gust that is wandering overhead, as well as to
catch up the rollicking blast that follows the
floor of the country. Not a tree, nor a shrub,
scarcely even a furze-mote, or a stub of dead
ground-oak, varies with a looser twang the per-

petually tense wail of the wind on granite—a
tone too dismal, and too dreary, for echo, or
description.

Gruff Howell was sleeping, like a lawyer's
conscience, richly, and without prejudice. He
never went to bed much, but achieved his rest,
like a warrior on a tomb, with his clothes on.

To-night, the wind was scarcely even keeping
itself in practice; and the moon was having
an unusual turn of insight into the *Raven*.
All around the hills were silent; and the long
pale shadows lay, like flaws of calm on tidal
waters; while the " holy circles," where unholy
deeds had stained the moor, stood up, like
ghosts that have no churchyard. Only the
solemn bird, that watches the dim night for a
century, and times its slow watches with a
croak, was moving, uneasily. moving his long
gaunt body, with the platform of his frayed nest
waiting in the crag, for him to mend.

Suddenly the poor old mastiff-bitch, who
wandered round the house at night, gave three
sharp yelps, and made a spring; but receiving a blow on the nose fell back, and in that
position became qualified to digest a kick in the
stomach. Then a storm of thumps broke upon
the hob-nailed door, and a mighty noise rang

through the house; till the master looked out of the window, with an oath, and pointed a long gun at his own porch. "Come down," said a stern voice; and down he went, while his wife shivered worse than at fifty burglars.

Old Griffith Howell now was longing, as his wife sincerely hoped, to turn a new leaf of his life, to cast away the works of darkness, brew his own beer, and give no credit. For since the penny-post came in, the heavens had blessed him with a great surprise. He had heard of his only son, a soldier, long astray in foreign parts, and long despaired of in home quarters; and without falling under proper average of reason, he placed such a piece of news entirely to the credit of the penny-post. And this made him pay attention now to the doings of his visitor.

"The candle is enough. Rake the fire together, and put a block of dry peat on. Go for the loaf, and the streaky bacon, and the sharp knife with the heel to it. Very well. This packet is for me, with urgency? Leave me to consider it, while you see to the victualling. Don't draw the ale, till I tell you, mind. When my supper is ready, you may go to bed again."

With these words, the man of the sheep-skins, looking thoroughly weary, sat heavily down at the oaken board set up for a table; with a jerk of his thumb, he broke the seal of the letter, which Howell had given him, and read it by the grimy yellow light. And though he was glad to find little to do, his nasty temper made him grumble at it.

" Child's work—mere child's work—an insult to me," he muttered, while Howell went fumbling about; " even the forgery all done to hand, and directions, as if I were a stupid errand-boy. 'Put this slip in with the opened letter, seal with the seal enclosed, and post it, but not at Christowell, to-morrow.' Very good; very well; it shall be done, sir; as the fates have made you my master for the present; though you don't catch me going near a post-office. No sham civilization for me. I have taken to the moor, and mean to stick to it."

CHAPTER XVII.

ON THE BRINK, AND OVER IT.

IGNORANT of all plots against him, and even of
any occasion for them, Captain Larks was pro-
ceeding steadily, with the garden-labours of the
year. For May is a month of urgent call, and
claim, from every rooted being, whether from
under the blurred and mottled sky, which man
spreads over them, or from beneath the clearer
blue of nature's glazing only. This is the time,
to rise right early, to breathe crisp air, and
tread fresh earth, and do brisk work, that shall
brighten up the heart, with beauty, and with
goodly relish, in the by-and-by of resting.

Shall we be content, to maunder, and to let
the right hand flag, among the many works
that claim it, for no better reason than some
trivial flout within ourselves? Somebody has
run down our work; some boy has thrown a
stone, and sped away rejoicing; some jealous

brother of the spade declares, that we are but a tinkling cymbal; worst of all, some foe has darkly re-assessed us, when we paid three times too much already—yet all these woes, though a single day inflict them, shall not stay the true hand, one half-hour.

" I find it like this," said Captain Larks, as he set his heel firmly on a leather-coated grub, " that if I begin to think, think I may, and be nowhere at all, but only grow 'weist,' as they call it about here, instead of growing wise. But if I begin to work, there I am; something to show, and something to grow ; and a thankful heart, and a peaceful spirit. Now for the last, and the maddest of my crazes, according to some of the wiseacres; though in bare fact, a great success already."

Has there ever been a craze, that was not a great success, in the opinion of the crazy one ? Not that the captain deserved to be so called, by reason of his present crotchet; for verily there was good sense in it, as well as small risk, and much beautiful amusement. What he wanted to establish, was an English vineyard ; the which used to flourish many centuries ago, and is to be heard of, every now and then, as flourishing here and there, down to the present time ; with taste, skill, and money, and good luck, to help it.

Bacchus loves the hills, as the ancient writers tell us ; and yet he detests rough mountain winds.   Let a nook be found for him, with crag enough to shelter, and sun enough to warm his graceful curls, and soil enough to feed his juicy growth ; then let human skill nurse him daily, human force scatter his countless foes, and Fortune and Providence alike smile on him—and in a fine season, there may be some sour grapes.

Here, beneath the rough crest of the moor, the home and shelter had been found, the nurture of light shelf-land, and reflected warmth of sun, whenever he came out.   However there had been no grapes as yet ; but nothing could be simpler than the reason—they were not going to begin too soon.   " Everybody knows," said Mr. Arthur, " what is the consequence of allowing the vine to fruit prematurely.   Eager young people, like my daughter Rose, may long to see a dozen bunches upon every vine, before the stem is thicker than a knitting needle.   But that is not my system, sir."

The third season's growth was now beginning ; and the sight was very pretty to a gardening mind.   For a nook of cliff, perpendicular above, and shelfing at the bottom, had been well fenced off, so as to help the native curtain of the rock, in fending the summer gale; and also to shut out wandering pigs, and gormandizing cows, and the graceless sheep, without even a horn to drag him to the altar by. And now, in the shelter of their sloping nest, more than three hundred maiden vines were peeping at the prospect of the sky. Whether should they come out of bud, throw forth another joint of growth, with a heel of leaf to stand upon, and a comb (like the fringes of a moth) to go on with; or whether should they abide a wee bit longer, within the golden eider of their mantles; and thus reserved give the sun to understand, that his meaning was kind and cordially welcome, but not yet established against white frost. Some did the one thing, and some did the other; according to the impetuosity of sap.

What a pleasure it is, to see a man look happy! Partly, no doubt, because that pleasure is so rare. But now Captain Larks, with his leathern apron on, and leather behind him for to sit upon, and a great many pockets full of everything he wanted, sat down among his vines, and did look happy. For these came along the ground, not ramping upward, neither flabbing downward with a dissolute redundancy; but curt, and vigorous, and robust, with every joint as ripe as a boiled ox-tail. Like the fingers of a star, they were spread above the earth, led horizontally to catch ground heat, at a height of about nine inches; and a man might sit upon the ground among them, and lift his head, as in an orchestra of fiddling, and thank the Lord, who made him, for the better music here.

"Father, I tell you, once more, that you are too bad, when you get into this dreadful corner," young Rose almost shouted out; so jealous was she of this little vineyard, in which she was not allowed to work as yet, because she did not understand it; "and I assure you, without exaggeration, that I must have been half an hour looking for you; and here you are, just as if nobody ever had serious business to attend to!"

"Well, let us have the serious business. I see a great deal too serious here." The captain had found five snails stuck together, looking into one another's windows, as they will.

"I intend to come up; though I dare say you don't want me," cried Rose, as she gathered in her skirts, and stepped lightly; "there now, I have not even frightened a bud. You will have to call me in, to help you soon, jealous as you are, dear father. Now my news is, that a gentleman is come, who wants leave to fish in our little stream, so please you."

"I can't attend to him now; and I can't have him flogging away, through my pear-trees. Don't you see, that I have got nearly thirty bushels of old tan, to spread along the ground, before these vines are one day older? And all to do myself—every bit of it, myself. I can't have clumsy fingers here. Tell him to go, and fish some other river."

"That would be a nice thing for me to say, papa, to a gentleman who caught me up, when the horse knocked me down so, at Moreton."

"Rose, sometimes you are quite as provoking, as a full-grown married woman. Was I to know, by instinct, who this man is? If he has been kind to you, he may fish for ever. Tell him so, with my compliments; and say that when he has done, I shall hope to see, and thank him. But fishermen never want to be disturbed."

"Like certain other people, who are too busy to be mentioned. This gentleman's name is

'Washton,' I believe; and he wants some trout for a sick lady. If it were not for that, he never would have taken the liberty of asking leave."

"Fishermen always want fish for sick ladies. And they mainly take the liberty, of not asking leave. However, let him fish, to his heart's content, if he doesn't hook my pear-trees. I dare say, he doesn't know a trout from a Forelle."

"If he gets a good catch, you shall have a dish for supper. I shall watch him in the distance; I love to watch a fisherman; his looks are solid wisdom."

"Short is the only man, who can make head, or tail, of the fish in this water; but let Mr. Washton try his hand, my darling. A very sick lady could eat more than he will catch to-day."

"He looks as if he could fish well," said Rose, hastening with bright cheeks, and brilliant eyes —for she still was a child when excited—to authorize, and behold the sport, if any.

"Don't rob him of his fish, you greedy little creature," her father shouted after her, down the vineyard hollow; "let the sick lady have every one he catches."

Rose kissed her hand, to show that she would be obedient; and then at a very nimble pace set off, with her slender form glancing in and out of tender foliage, towards the bottom of the meadow, sacred to the good cow " Mopsy."

For here it was, that she had been at work, and singing pleasantly, weaving a disc of prim-rose-buds, with purple shade of violets, when a fishing-rod came through the hedge, and a hat full of amazement after it. " You have made a mistake," said Rose, looking as calmly as Mopsy at him, " this is my father's property. We are very particular about our fences."

The ingenuous youth betrayed much confu-sion, or at any rate tried to do so; and tried very cleverly, with the stern truth against him —that he knew all these things, and now was here, in virtue of that knowledge.

" How stupid I am! I beg a thousand par-dons," he answered with profound humility; " but I thought these moorland streams were free. But I see that there is a most lovely place here—a gentleman's private residence. Forgive me; I was thinking of a lady who is ill; and I wanted a few trout so sadly."

" Don't go away, you shall have them," said Rose; " if I can find my father; and if you can catch them."

With admirable patience, he had waited,

gazing into the desired land, and envying the Christow at leisure straying through it, the cow, that could come up, and breathe on Rose's shoulder, and even the grass, that such a blessed cow made milk of. For verily, this young man was stricken with a great and lifelong blow, from simply opening his arms, and finding a maiden there, in the street of Moreton. No mere flash of fancy, or dazzle of sight, or sparkle of admiration, but a deep and high power of a larger existence than his own, and a rapture of ennoblement. For a week, he had seemed to be walking in a dream, and his tongue had turned white, though he used it very sparingly. There was no cure for him, but a hair of the dog—but out upon such low metaphors!

Now, as he sat upon the bank, outside of his Paradise, pretending to be busy with his fly-book, he espied, through a neat little peep-hole of twigs, the maiden of his heart coming back to him. And being at such a respectful distance, he was not afraid to watch her; which the bashfulness of love prevented him from doing at close quarters. Surely, there never was till now a form so graceful, a walk of such sweetly flowing elegance, a poise of the head so delicate and maidenly—ah, now she was coming, and he could not look! He would wait for the heavenly music of her voice.

"Plaise, sir, be 'e the young man, as wor axing lave, vor to vish in this here watter?"

The capricious Rose had stopped at home, and sent Moggy to represent her. Jack Westcombe was so vexed, that he scarcely cared to answer, but jumped up, and stared at Moggy, with cheeks even redder than her own.

"'Cos if 'e be," said Moggy, "Cappen zeth 'e be kindly welcome. And a' will come and look arter 'e, for fraid of 'e kitching of our vroot plantesses."

This little addition was of Moggy's own invention; for she said to herself—"Where be the young chap's manners? A' standeth there like a stuck pig, as if I wor a Bartlemy!" Then off she walked, with a sharp toss of her head, and a strong impress of heels upon the soft grass of the meadow. She considered herself a very pretty girl; and she liked other people to agree with her.

Westcombe's mind was as reasonable perhaps, as any mind can hope to be, at the age of three-and-twenty; and he might have been sure, that no gentleman would have sent him that rude message. At first however, he turned round in dudgeon, and began to take the fly-collar off his fishing-line; and if there had not been a hitch about this, his life might have hung upon a very different loop. But when a man is in a hurry, (and for certain, if his hurry be knotted with wrath,) every little thing that can converge to a confluence of tangles, rushes into every kind of complication, with a subtlety that proves the multiplicity of the devil.

Now many young fellows would have gnashed their teeth, pulled out a seven-bladed knife, and slashed away. But Jack was gifted with a turn of obstinacy, equal to any ingenuity of gut; and instead of growing pettish, he became more calm, while he worked with his fingers ex-pediently. Presently, this patience and consideration spread from his fingers to his mind, through that sympathy between them, which compels the mind to clench the fingers, when it waxes wrathful. And thus he began to see the folly, and the littleness of taking offence, where none is offered.

"The captain is fond of his little joke, perhaps," he said to himself, taking up his rod again; "and probably he agrees with Dr. Johnson, in the greatest mistake of that great bear. Never mind, I shall go on, and take my chance.

Possibly, I may see somebody again ; or at any rate, I may think of her."

It happened to be both the hour, and the day, when fish with one accord begin to feed. The eldest, truest, and deepest chip of the ancient block of Zebedee (who is pretty sure, even in these tumble-down times, to be of Apostolical succession), however shrewd his study of the loaves, and fishes, cannot predict when the fish will want their loaf, but is ready to present them with the hook, upon demand. The water is the same, and the weather has not changed ; to the keenest human eye and sense, there is no sign of difference ; yet certain it is, that for hours together, no trout will even look at the very finest fare ; and then all of a sudden, as if the dinner-bell rang, off scampers every trout to his private napkin-ring, wags his tail, and fans his fins, and goes up and down, like a Corporation saying grace.

Westcombe was not at all a mighty dab at angling. That noble absorption of all conscious existence, upon the behaviour of a small cock's hackle, that absolute devotion of entire brain, and heart, to the humours of a slippery speckle, just beginning to outgrow a tadpole—those high and wondrous powers of nature, which turn a

man into a fisherman, had not been vouchsafed
to this young fellow. However, he could throw
a fly very neatly, and pull out a fish, when the
hook stuck in him; and elated with unusual
success, he worked away, to surpass all pre-
vious record. And at least a score of trout
were considering, with gasps, the texture of a
Plymouth basket, by the time that he came to
the captain's drawbridge, and doubted about
going higher up the stream. For here were
flower-beds, and pretty walks of gravel, and pet
places looked upon by modest cottage-windows.

Fearing to trespass upon favour, he turned at
this point, and began considering. Beyond
doubt, a dish of fish was due to the good owner,
together with the decency of thanks for his permission. And yet it would be an awkward
thing, to march up to the door, knock, and
introduce himself, and seem to want to disturb
the captain in his well-known retirement. So
he thought, that he would fish his way back
again down stream and find perhaps some workman, or some messenger to send. He forgot
that the weather, which makes trout feed (un-
accountably, as aforesaid) has a thoroughly
national, and rational effect, upon the British
workman, despatching him, without delay, to

the happy realms of slumber.   The only failure of accord between them, was that Sam Slowbury felt the weather, even more promptly than the trout, and had his mouth wide open for the flies, five minutes before theirs were ready.   At a corner of the brook, about an hour ago, the fisherman either heard, or seemed to hear, a very loud sound in the distance of the land, regular, and to some extent harmonious; which he took for the roaring of a bull upon the moor.

"At it again!   It is really too bad," suddenly Jack Westcombe heard a lively voice pronouncing; "an hour and a half, is his allowance after dinner; and now he must have been four hours at it, solidly; not to mention all his little dozes on his shovel.   Rose, if you insist upon my keeping such a fellow, I shall call upon you to pay his wages."

"But think of all the very small Slowburies, papa.   And if he is not very quick, remember, how thoroughly good-natured, and quiet he is."

"Quiet indeed!   Do you call that quiet?   I call it the very loudest snore I ever heard. And here is the gentleman fishing.   I was coming to look for you, and thank you, Mr. Washton, for your kindness to my dear child the other day.   Don't think me ungrateful for having been so long. I expected to have seen you further up, long since; and being very busy, I forgot how time goes by. You might have filled your basket, up the brook, by this time. I heard the trout leaping there continually."

" Oh, thank you, I have done quite as well as I could wish. I fear that you will think me very greedy, when you see them. I am sure, I am very much obliged to you, sir. May I go to your door, and leave a few with the servant? I have had famous sport, much more than enough for my dear mother, and all of us."

With these words Jack Westcombe leaped up the bank, as gracefully as stiff legs could do it— for the sake of Rose—and with a brave bow, but a very timid glance at her, spread the contents of his basket at her feet. There was not a fish of more than half a pound among them; but still they made a handsome show, by reason of their number.

"Many of the poor things are alive," cried Rose ; " surely you don't let them die so slowly? I suppose it is their nature to be caught; but still—— "

" Nine fishermen out of ten do it," said the captain; for he saw that his visitor was troubled, and surprised ; " but a touch in the right place saves them pain ; and what is more important from the human point of view, they are crisper in the pan from the happy despatch. But they are a pretty lot. You must be a skilful angler. Our trout are very hard to catch, I know. A friend of mine says, that they are like the ladies. Sometimes they won't look at you ; and then again—but never mind. He is an ancient bachelor."

Westcombe stole a clever glance at Miss Arthur, to ask what her opinion was upon this question ; but being a diffident young maiden, she looked down, and began to count the trout sedately. Just at the moment, when she was doing this, opening and closing her rosy lips, like a school-girl doing arithmetic, and jogging one finger at every little fish, the westerly sun, gliding out from a cloud, glanced over the dance of the water, and through a tissue of young leaves upon her. The sweetness and innocence of her face were lit up, like an opening rose ; every delicate line, and soft clear colour of the perfect oval, was enlivened with thoughtful pleasure, kind will, and the bloom of faith in everything ; while the power of loving, as none but women can love, waited in the clear depth of her eyes.

"Now don't be greedy, Rose, my dear," Mr. Arthur said, with a truly parental, and prosaic turn of thought, which set young Westcombe's teeth on edge, for his rapturous gaze had sealed his fate; "not one of those fish shall you have for supper, though you long to exhibit your frying powers. We thank you heartily, Mr. Washton; but we can always have them when we like. Pack them all again, in your basket. Rose, there are many things for you to do. This gentleman will excuse you."

In a moment, the light of the world was gone, with a curtsy, from Jack Westcombe's eyes; and he began to put his poor fish away, with a very gloomy air.

"You must not think," said the captain, observing his manner with surprise, "that I am ungrateful; but I wish you to have a good dish; and as I said, we can always get them. From the freshness of the water, the Christow trout are as good on the third day as on the first; or better, according to a friend of mine. You are welcome to fish here, whenever you like. Will you come up to the cottage, and taste my cider? We have a very decent ham in cut."

"The thought is very kind. But I have far

to go ; and the moon will not be up till late to-night. I will thank you once more, and say ' good-bye.' "

Mr. Arthur, by this time, was so ingrained to the pleasures of a lonely life (which are the most trustworthy) that he was generally glad to say, " good-bye." But the young man lingered, and looked at him ; and observing him now for the first time closely, the elder took a liking to him. In spite of wide philosophy, and vast philanthropy, most of us like, or dislike, at first touch.

" I want to tell you one thing," said young Westcombe, blushing deeply, and with the full sense of it, looking firmly at the man he spoke to ; " it was not the fishing, that I came for. I came in the hope of seeing Miss Arthur. Because—because I never yet saw anybody like her. You have been kind to me ; and I should be a sneak, if I did not tell you."

" What ! " cried the captain ; " do you mean my Rose ? "

" I mean the young lady, who has been here with us. The only young lady in the whole world to me. The one who sprang out, into the middle of the road, before a mad horse, to save a baby, without a single thought of her own dear life. And by the most wonderful presence of mind, she saved the baby; but the Lord alone saved her. You look, as if I were exaggerating."

"Her account of the matter was entirely different." Mr. Arthur spoke coldly; but the quick warmth of pride in his daughter flushed his cheeks and brow.

"Of course it was. She made it out to be nothing. Her nature would compel her to do that," Westcombe exclaimed, as if he knew the maiden, ten times better than her father did; "my dear sir, I saw the whole of it, although I was too far off to stop it; and I tell you there never was a grander thing done, by any one so young, and so beautiful."

"I scarcely see how that last point bears upon the merits of the exploit," Mr. Arthur answered, with a little of the bluntness, which always comes of solitude; "however, I am glad to hear, that my daughter did her duty."

"It was not her duty. It is no one's duty, to risk a precious life in that way. I beg your pardon, for going on about it. The difference is, that I saw it, and you hear of it. And because there was no fuss made about it, you think that I exaggerate."

"I think nothing of the kind. I know the nature of my child. And I thank you, sir, for valuing it. Also I thank you, for your manly truth, and honesty, in telling me what has brought you here. But I grieve to say—because I like you, and you remind me of a dear old friend—that you must not come here any more."

"I hope, sir,—I beg of you," the young man answered, noticing the kind, but resolute, look of the elder, with a wistful glance, "not to think ill of me, because I came this morning under false pretences. I never did anything like that before; and now that I think of it, I am quite ashamed. I tried to do without it, and really fought against it. But ever since that day at Moreton, I have not been like myself."

"I forgive you most freely for that little crime," Mr. Arthur replied with a hearty smile: "it was nothing but a young man's trick. Another thought would have put a stop to it."

"Then why am I to come no more? I will pledge my honour, to do nothing underhanded. I tell you the truth. I shall never care for any one in all the world, except your daughter.

It will make no difference in my feelings, if I have to wait fifty years for her. At the same time, I beg to state, that I hope to get her sooner; but without attempting anything outside your knowledge. I know well enough, that I am not to be compared with her, in any of the higher attributes. And I know her too well, to suppose that she would think twice of any of the lower ones. But for all that, I am not going to be discouraged. My father never meant a thing, without going through with it. And I am as like him as two peas; though not to be compared with him, for goodness."

"Your father must have been a peculiar gentleman, if you resemble him in character."

"My father is living, sir, and not at all peculiar. Unless it is peculiar, to be brave and upright, generally admired, and universally beloved. He is not known yet, upon this side of Dartmoor; but everybody knows him in the western parts; and his name will last for ever, in the history of the war. You may have heard of Colonel Westcombe."

"What a wooden brain I have!" thought Mr. Arthur, sitting down, to hide a change of countenance; "so much stooping dims perception. He is the very image of his father, though taller, and stronger, and better looking. Once and for all, it must be stopped."

Meanwhile Jack was looking brightly at him, and saying to his hopeful heart—"Come now! I put it very mildly; but it must tell for something."

"My daughter told me that your name was 'Washton;' and she very seldom makes mistakes." Mr. Arthur went into this side-issue, partly perhaps to get time for thinking.

"The Moreton people, when they found my name out," Jack replied, with a quiet smile, "made 'Wasshcum' of it, with a sharp a, as in 'cash,' according to their manner of pronouncing. And so, I dare say, it got into 'Washton.' We seem to speak better, upon our side of the moor. You should come over, and hear us, sir."

"I fear there is no chance of it. You are a very young man; and I shall very soon be an old one. It would grieve me that your father's son, or indeed that any gentleman, should have reason to believe me churlish. I will tell you, if you will promise to keep what I tell you in strict confidence, even from your father, why you must never come here more."

"I will give you my honour, sir, not to speak of it to any one."

"Thank you; I know that I can trust you. The reason is simply this. Very strange circumstances, which I must not enter into, have made it the first duty of my life, to obliterate myself entirely—to conceal my existence—to desire to be dead, except for one pure precious sake. While I live in this way, my child must do the same. Not that I shall sacrifice her better life to mine. If she gives her heart to any one, and he is worthy of her, they shall not find me an obstacle. But as yet, she is too young to judge, or even think of it. And I have a right to keep her to myself, and to live as the story of my life demands; until my child's welfare compels me to do otherwise. I see that you clearly understand me."

"I am trying to do so," the young man answered, with a very dismal gaze at him; "and I am sure, that I am very much obliged to you, for trying to explain it. But I cannot see, why I should be forbidden to come any more, if I do no harm, and do not even see the young lady. It seems very hard, as you must acknowledge. Even to see the house where she lives, and to get a glimpse of your hat, without coming near you, would be the greatest comfort to me, and give me some idea of kindness. I am sure, that you have known my father, sir, from the manner of your eyes just now; and I never yet met anybody, who had known him, without liking him."

"You are right, my lad, I have known your father well," Mr. Arthur answered warmly; "and a nobler man I never knew; and that is why I trust you. The greatest mistake in the world is, to allow, when once the mind is made up, a middle course. And I will have nothing of that sort now. But if it will do you any good, or ease your mind, to be upon my premises now and then, for the purpose of catching a fish or two, I am not sure that I should prosecute you. Only, of course, you must confine yourself strictly to your angling; and only come just now and then, at considerable intervals; and feel yourself entirely on your honour, when you do come."

"I thank you with all my heart, and I will observe your conditions strictly. I shall make a point of never coming more than once a week, and of never intruding on your pleasure-grounds. And if I ever send a few fish to the house, it shall be quite anonymous, and by the man that snores so. You have taken a great weight off my mind; and I tell you fairly, that I mean to hope; but nothing whatever shall be done, I mean, of course, upon your own place, without your entire knowledge." Jack Westcombe tried to wring the captain's hand, but got rather the worst of that; for of all things potting is most hardening.

CHAPTER XVIII.

WET, AND DRY.

LIKE every other ancient faith, the angler's firm belief, that fish refuse all food with rain impending, has now been scattered to the wind and clouds. The opinion of many ages was, that having by instinct surer knowledge, than all mankind by science get, of the things that shall occur to-morrow, these finny sages fear to spoil their relish for the coming treat of worms, and slugs, and grubs, more luscious than the fattest " native," to unvitiated taste. All these will fall into their mouths to-morrow; let them fast, to keep the feast.

It is now denied by men of science—scornful of all reasoning beyond their own—that a trout surpasses them so immensely, in the science of meteorology; of which they are bound to confess that they know nothing. And feeling some reasonable doubt of that denial, they add the insidious remark (engendered by their own "inner consciousness") that even if the fish knew what was coming, they would never keep their mouths shut, by reason of their knowledge.

Be that as it will, one thing is certain, the liberal rise of the Christow fish to the hook of Jack Westcombe did not preclude a heavy rain from setting in, next morning. Whoever has the pleasure of an intimate acquaintance—and in such a case there truly is no superficial knowledge—with a genuine hearty Dartmoor rain, will be ready to admit, that it has some meaning. Its main point of difference from most other rains is, that it combines all their bad qualities, and omits their good ones. However, to abuse it, only makes it rain the harder.

To prove that he was "game," and to celebrate becomingly his "most Providential restoration,"—as Lady Touchwood called it—young Squire Dicky had prepared an expedition against the rats of Dartmoor, transcending his defeated invasion, as largely as the armament of Xerxes surpassed that of Darius. A *triduum* of solid combat, (such as Greeks and Romans had, but civilized armies now eschew,) was ordered to begin, upon this great morning; for Dicky's `heart needed some repose from love; but lo, the very terriers, best waterproofed with wire, bore upon their flanks such bars, as the young of the salmon tribe have, or a race-horse after a heavy gallop; and such as no washing may produce upon a dog, nor anything else but a thick, steady rain, that hits them against, and up, the grain of their dear coats, and so pursues them, until their sweet skins become oozy.

Now Dr. Perperaps, beyond emphasis, and therefore in a whisper which outwent voice, had ordered, that the thing of all things his precious patient must most avoid, was the very slightest damp.

" And it ain't slight damp;" said Dicky, in his slang way, to his darling mother, as she told him this; "my name's ' ratter,' this juicy day, and no mistake. Find the beggars all at home, this weather. I've got my army ready, and I mean to march. Old Dr. Perperaps went on about 'slight damp;' but he never said a word against such heavy wet as this. Hi there, you fellows, I'll be down in a jiffy."

In a jiffy, he was down, but not as he intended; for his mother, being ample, and of very hearty substance, laid one strong arm across his back, and the other in the hollow of his knees; and thus having whisked him off his feet, bore him right easily to his bed-room, laid him on his bed, and locked him in. Then she sent orders to his army, to march to the brew-house, and have some beer, and a shilling apiece, and retire to their tents, until the next fine morning.

When the whole expedition was thus disbanded, Dicky was released; and recovering quickly from his indignation—for he never bore resentment long — he sauntered to his sister Julia's room, to tease her pet dog *Elfie*, and to talk about matters of importance, as he called them.

"Judy, shove aside your daubs," he said, for she was just pointing up, with fine grey eyebrows, a spirited sketch of Colonel Westcombe; "I want to consult you about a thing, that men cannot be expected much to enter into. I have already informed you, that my affections at last are permanently engaged."

"So they always are. To a new one, every month. Be constant, Dicky, this time, if you can; for I rather like Spotty Perperaps."

"What a pest you are! The spotty little fright! I am two inches taller than she is. Five feet four is the extreme lowest measure, as we say at Cambridge, of any girl I ever should make up to. You are such a height that you don't care. In fact, you had better have some short fellow ; if you are not too proud to have anybody."

" How does this bear upon your permanent affections ? "

" In this kind of way; as you ought to know, if your reasoning process was like ours. I scout the idea of Spotty Perperaps ; and I love Rose Arthur."

" Very well, let it be so. It is no concern of mine. Nothing ever comes of your adorations. The last was for a hideous bull-terrier. And probably the next will be for a badger."

" Judy, I came for your advice ; and not to be scoffed at with nasty levity. You thoroughly understand women, because you have got all their dodges in your nature. And all I ask you is a very simple thing—how would you recommend me to go on ? "

" I have never seen the girl. How can I tell you ? " Miss Touchwood answered, with large contempt. " Boys, like you, have a weak idea that all the women in the world are just alike, and as utter fools as they are themselves. I can only say this,—if you want to get on, be as unlike yourself as possible.

"If you had tried for an hour, even you could hardly have said a more nasty thing. It makes me wonder, when I come across nice girls, whether they would talk like you, after they got married. It makes one afraid to have anything to do with them. Nobody can have a finer nature than I have; but nothing ever comes of it."

" A very fine nature is its own reward," said Julia, touching up Colonel Westcombe. " But, Dicky, it never talks about itself."

" Very well. Let it do anything it pleases. I never stand up to be wonderful at all; but every man who keeps a dog is fond of me. And if all the girls think that I am to be got, by snubbing me, they will find themselves in the wrong box."

" Surely," said Julia, who after all was jealous, at hearing so much of Rose Arthur, " your new angel does not snub you, as if you did not even keep a dog."

" That is the very point," answered Dicky, coming up, and showing many blue pricks in one leg ; " these things made her take a liking to me; and I made the very most of them, tearing every hole that I could find, as game as if I meant to die for it. And for a long time, that scored three, every time I frightened her. But when I began to have Guinness, and to put one leg across the other, she seemed very suddenly to lose faith, and to think that I ought to put my boots on."

"Then she showed some sense, and I respect her for it. What a plague you must have been! Even when you are well, you can't stay still. And I dare say, you danced one foot all day. And you cannot say a word, about anything but vermin. How can you expect a pretty girl to like you?"

"It does not matter about that. They do," Dicky replied, as one who cites a fact, in lieu of argument; "I believe that it has something to do with this, that they think they can have their own way with me. That is the first thing all you women want. But she is very different from all you common females. Her mind is exalted, and her thoughts are large."

"It is a delight to hear that," Miss Touchwood answered, without leaving off her work; "because it might be a very awkward thing, if she were to consider you worth catching. Gossip is entirely below my notice. But the rather haughty gentleman—I suppose he is a gentleman—who calls himself ' Captain Larks,' lies under some cloud of mystery, at present. Of course, it may be nothing; but you know as well as I do, that many people say he is a criminal in hiding. Very likely that is rubbish. But till something more is known, the less we have to do with them, the better."

" Such nonsense drives me wild. What do you know of the world? You wanted to patronize Mr. Arthur—who never yet called himself Captain anything, and cares not a rap what fools say of him—and he put you down very neatly, and completely, simply by his manner, and without a word. It was a bitter pill for you, Miss Judy. But a bit of humble-pie every day, would do you good. The captain is the kindest man that ever lived. Many people think me a softy, and a fool. And I don't stick up to be a wonder. But I do know when people have been good to me, and put themselves out of their way, to help me. And I tell you, you are not fit to dust their floor for them. Put that in your pipe, and smoke it."

With this elegant counsel, Squire Dicky ran away, stopping both ears, as if to keep out wicked language ; while his sister only smiled, for she loved to irritate him, but never allowed him to do the like to her. But she could not help thinking of his very frank remarks, about her own character, and wondering whether there might be a grain of truth at the bottom of them.

"Hurrah! Here comes somebody! A plucky cove, whoever he may be," shouted the excitable Dicky, in the "corridor"—as Lady Touchwood loved to call it; "Judy, shut up your lozenge-box, as soon as you have put a little lake upon your cheeks. I was just going to send to the stable for a halter! But here comes a visitor, to ruin the new velvet. Her ladyship will be in a precious state of mind. I defy him to sit down, without a quart of drainage. And the new peach-colour runs, if a fellow sneezes in the next room."

Her ladyship however was a match for the emergency. The front-door bell had not ceased clanging, ere the much keener jingle of her own was heard, and the footman knew well which required first attention. "The little study, James, whoever it is! And put the big Bible open in the easy-chair, first." The man understood, made the only cushioned chair pretty safe from invasion; and then showed in Mr. Short.

"Capital device! I give her credit for it," said the vicar to himself, while the man went to announce him.

"Now I do call this very good of you indeed," Lady Touchwood exclaimed, without a bit of falsehood, as she came in, and made her sleeve go up, in a manner understood by women only, for fear of his fingers having dribbles to them; "an otter, or an oyster, or a conger-eel, is the only thing fit to be out, on such a day."

"I rather like it;" said the parson, with a countenance which did not express any very keen delight, except such as a joint may find in basting; "at any rate, no weather ever stops me, except such a snow as we had, two years ago. You sent for me urgently; and I was bound to come."

"No. I have not sent for you. It has been raining, I cannot say how long. Would I dream of sending for you, in such weather? I never do anything outrageous."

"I thought you might have boxed—the compass in such weather. Here is your letter, your own handwriting—though the ink may have run, with more rain, than sand upon it."

" There is both rain, and sand upon it," the lady answered, drawing back both hands ; " but I never wrote a word of it. You know that I never use sand now. I keep it in the ink-stand ; but I scarcely ever use it, except from habit, when I happen to forget. This is not my writing. At what time did you get it ? "

" About twelve o'clock. Trickey leaves my letters to the last, because of these boots you see. I will tell you that, another time. What you say makes me a little uncomfortable. I could have sworn, this was your handwriting."

" It not only is not my handwriting, but it is a very clumsy imitation of it. And do I put it this way—'Lady Touchwood presents her compliments to Mr. Short '—after all the years that I have known, and liked you ? "

" I know that you never begin like that ; except when something has put you out. But excuse my remembering, that you did write so, about six months back, when I had vexed you. And I thought that you might have been annoyed again, though I could not call to mind my fault. And that made me order my horse at once ; for I had some idea—but never mind that."

Mr. Short's futile idea had been, that Lady

Touchwood must have discovered, at last, his admiration of her daughter; and this had brought him straightway, to face the question.

"That letter was posted at our post-office, and in one of those horrid new envelopes," the lady proceeded, with that calm judgment which we all exert, upon the troubles of our friends; "you may depend upon it, that you have been decoyed from home, for some bad purpose. Either to rob you on your road, or to rob your house, while you were away. Everybody says how rich you are."

"It is good to have the highest of all characters. Since you have not sent for me, and do not want me in this morassy state; I will say 'good-morning,' Lady Touchwood."

"You shall do nothing of the sort, until you have had one of those long twisted glasses (from some undiscovered country) of my white-currant cordial. There is no Mrs. Short to look after you, or to reproach me for not doing so." Lady Touchwood gave a sly glance herewith, for she was much too sharp, not to know of his weakness for Julia, and had no fear of it. "But you came through the rain, to oblige me, as you thought; and you are frightfully soaked; and riding home you will have the wind on your back, and get lumbago. You know my patent cordial, don't you? None of your currant wine—oh, Lord!—but the very finest whisky and white currants, done by a very old receipt, and bottled to stand upright for at least seven years."

"It sounds very good. But shall I stand upright, or sit upright in the saddle, with the wind upon my back, and lumbago coming? I will take nothing more than a glass of your old ale, the golden ale made of the Wiveliscombe malt; and then I will ask your good son Dicky, for one of his long old tough cigars. With the wind on the crupper, it will last me all the way."

These things were sent for, and the horse was ordered (much against his liking, for he was just doing nicely), and then Lady Touch-wood took the opportunity of putting a word in season, just at the genial moment of good relish, which a fine ham-sandwich gives to ale. "And how is Captain Larks getting on?" said she. "Everything he does is so delightful. When will you bring him over?"

"As soon as he will come," replied the wary parson. "Why should I hurry him? Am I bound to commit social suicide? I feel myself cast into the shade already, because there is no romance about me."

" No, no, you are never in the shade," cried the lady, being dull at metaphor; " everybody knows every atom about you. He is the one, that is in the shade. But I am sure, that he never deserved it."

" He appears very honest, and he may be that," said the vicar, with a solemn shake of head; " but where did he get his silver spoons ? "

" Come now, you are a great deal too jealous." Lady Touchwood always supposed a person, who did not smile, to be in earnest. " If there is anything the matter with him, it must be at least of the upper classes. He has been accustomed to the best society. I am sure, he never would do anything, of a lower rank than forgery."

" Let us make a round-robin, and put in the middle—' Is it forgery, is it homicide, is it treason ? Your hearty well-wishers feel confident, that you have done something respectable.' If I prepare the document, will you sign it at the top ? "

" Go along. Here is your horse at the door. There never is any reasoning with you. But

I do hope that you will not catch cold, or find anything at home, to vex you."

"I am not afraid. My house can defy the world, with Mrs. Agget in it, and good *Nous* upon guard. Oh, here comes Squire Dicky, just in time to say 'good-bye.' How well he looks! Why, my good friend, glass and putty seem to suit your constitution. I must build a new greenhouse, for you to tumble through it."

"I am pretty sure of one thing; if I did, you would never be like Captain Arthur. You would make me pay for it, and for all the plants too."

"What a wise babe it is! He has hit the mark. Lady Touchwood, the Cantabs always do. But don't come out in the rain, my friend. Your glazing is not water proof."

"I hope he will find his old house robbed;" said Dicky, as the parson rode away, and the story of the letter was repeated. "It would be worth a hundred pounds to me, to have a rise taken out of him. He thinks himself so confoundedly clever; and he never lets another fellow say a single word almost."

"Now, don't be so spiteful, my dear. I am sure, that you always hold your own with him.

It amuses me sometimes, to hear you get so very much the better of him."

But Dicky shook his head. For he was a candid youth, and knew that he had no chance with Mr. Short, in any other view than his dear mother's.

END OF VOL. I.

LONDON: PRINTED BY WILLIAM CLOWES AND SONS, LIMITED,
STAMFORD STREET AND CHARING CROSS.